BLIND PATRIOT

PUPPET CONTROLS ANOTHER PUPPET

KUMAR PARAS

Contents

About Author

Kumar Paras is a young writer from India with an immense love for dystopian and politics themes. A high school student, he draws inspiration from his passion for literature, politics, and history, weaving complex narratives that challenge perspectives and provokes thought.

In addition to writing novels, he enjoys photography, sketching, and diving deep into historical and political issues, which often influence his storytelling. With *Blind Patriot*, he aims to explore a dystopian world of National Socialist Party of Parserland, while inviting readers to question the current world around them

Introduction

In the aftermath of the civil war that reshaped North Parserland under the authoritarian rule of the NSPP (National Socialist Party of Parsers), **Elias Vyane**, a loyal supporter of the regime, works as a spy to expose those conspiring against the government. However, when he uncovers the full extent of the NSPP's brainwashing machine, Elias is forced to question his loyalty filled with guilt, his faith in the regime, and the ideals he once held dear. Trapped between the corruption that taints every side, Elias must confront his greatest enemy—himself

Kumar Paras

.

Matorgoes1025@gmail.com

I
ENCOUNTER

The clock struck past 11 at night. It was August, yet in Parserland, winter always arrived early.

Elias walked down the snow-covered lane, speaking softly to the wind that trailed beside him like an old friend. In one hand, he held a lamp—flickering and faint—and in the other, a document containing vital evidence against the National Socialist Party.

The darkness was overwhelming. The lamp cast only a narrow circle of light, barely enough to see the path ahead.

Then a voice called out from behind.

"Elias Vyane."

He turned sharply, but the dim glow from the lamp wasn't enough to see clearly. All he could make out was a coat, a hat, and hair that looked eerily similar to his friend Thomas.

The figure stepped forward slowly, closing the distance.

"Who goes there?" Elias shouted, suspicion heavy in his voice.

But the figure didn't respond. It only repeated his name.

"Elias Vyane."

As it drew closer, the lamp's light finally revealed the face. Elias let out a sigh of relief.

Thomas.

He chuckled nervously. Maybe it was just one of Thomas's pranks again.

But Thomas didn't smile.

Instead, he raised his arm—revealing a pistol clenched tightly in his hand.

Elias' heart dropped. In that moment, time froze. Just a single squeeze of the trigger, and it would all be over—his past, his present... gone.

"I know what you're holding, comrade," Thomas said, his voice sharp and cold.

"Hand it over. Or I won't hesitate. One shot, and your blood will flow like the failed revolution of the South."

He took another step forward, unfazed.

"To me, the Party comes before everything. I'd die for our Supreme Leader—and kill for him too."

Elias didn't speak.

He slowly lowered the document into the snow. The wind howled louder. Snowflakes began piling on top of the exposed paper like nature itself trying to bury the truth.

He raised his hands in surrender.

There was nothing else to do.

And then—

Another figure approached from the dark...

II

WORK. WORK! WORK?

2 months earlier,

A fine summer day of June, a day after National Socialist Party of Parsers emerged victorious in the civil war. It was 4 a.m., the city was still shrouded in darkness—the usual time for Elias to wake up for his work.

The alarm blared: *"Work. Work! Work?"*

"The workers rise, the economy drives, the country thrives."

Elias always felt motivated by this as a loyal member of the NSPP. However, at times, it annoyed him. He turned off the alarm and proceeded towards the kitchen to prepare coffee.

The smell of coffee always brightened his day. With a cup in hand, he walked towards his balcony.

He noticed how quiet the city was. Slowly, the sun was defeating the darkness, with the clouds aiding in its victory. *"Where's the speaking machine? Ah! There it comes,"* murmured *Elias.* (The speaking machine is a typical propaganda vehicle used by the NSPP during the civil war.)

"Your Supreme Leader is working day and night—
For you, for your family,
For the country.
The glorious monument of the Supreme Leader will be
inaugurated today at the town square. You are all invited. I
repeat, you are all invited.
And always remember: "The workers rise, the economy
drives, the country thrives."

Elias felt enthusiasm and patriotism running through his veins. It was just a day after years of civil war had come to an end, and he heavily relied on the party to make this country rise from the ruins and shape their future. Soon he noticed his neighbor Comrade Cristo , who was standing on the balcony just beside Elias's, separated only by a small boundary. Cristo was also listening to the speaking machine but did not look excited, nor did he react to Elias's greeting. It wasn't a surprising moment, as Elias knew Comrade Cristo was secretly a Democrat supporter—probably disgusted by the news of the monument. Elias also recalled how Cristo had once accused the speaking machine of being nothing more than a propaganda tool.

Not wasting another minute, Elias wore his usual office coat with a sigh muttering under his breath about Cristo's foolishness but a sense of

Suspicion emerged *"What if Cristo is conspiring something against NSPP ?"*. Elias locked his house and, as usual, saw that the lift was under maintenance. He took the stairs beside the lift. He carefully navigated through the rubble of fallen buildings scattered across the streets. Finally, reached his office—where something he never expected awaited him.

III

OLD FRIEND

Elias was frozen, weeping at the sight of his friend after a long separation standing before the main office door.

"Good morning, comrade," Thomas said, stretching each word with a wide grin, as though he wanted to make up for lost time in that one moment.

"Thomas Harper... I thought I'd never see you again," Elias choked out, tears streaming as he stumbled over the words; his eyes, though, were weighed down with everything that he couldn't say out loud.

Elias had lost Thomas in the chaos of the civil war, one that he had long accepted to have been shot dead by some rogue Democrat.

"Ah, I am not leaving this world so easily, I suppose," Thomas laughed heartily. "You must have so many questions, right, Elias? Come, let's have a conversation over a cup of tea."

While they walked towards the tea corner, Elias observed how fabulously the office was decorated celebrating the victory of NSPP.

His eyes wandered about the party flags filling the space-- at the center a star, surrounded by white, and at the top a regal purple symbolizing the Supreme Leader guiding Parserland to its destiny, and at the bottom bold red representing the sacrifices of comrades in the great civil war.

It all looked like a dream, as he had always wanted the NSPP to win the war, but at the same time, it was frightening. The decorations reminded him of the years of struggle and the loved ones he lost in the conflict. However, he found himself constantly distracted by the unusual enthusiasm the office exuded-a sight that felt out of place.

Aroma of Tea ran through his veins. "Ah, if only I know how much I've missed this smell," Elias murmured to himself.

The speaking machine glanced into his office, giving the announcement again. "Your supreme leader is working day and…"

"Speaking machine, an invention that I think is perhaps one of the greatest", Thomas said proudly.

"without any doubt, I suppose," replied Elias.

Soon they reached the tea corner; Thomas sweetly rushed forward as he saw Missy serving tea that morning.

"Comrade Misty, give us a socialist special tea, will you?" Thomas smirked.

Oh, he's flirting with Misty again, as usual. It wasn't surprising: Thomas would always flirt with any lady he found attractive, Elias thought.

"I'm oh so happy to see you, Thomas. Feels like it's been a decade since I last saw you in the tea corner," replied Misty.

But by the way Misty rolled her eyes and with the blankness even on her face, anyone could easily catch that she was not interested in Thomas at all.

They would sit in the chairs by the window where the ruined city unfolded below them. The flag of the NSPP flew high above every building terrace. Far away, Elias could see the speaking machine moving near the bridge which connected East and West Parserland.

"Thomas Harper, so tell me how you survived those thirsty claws of the Democrats," inquired Elias, his voice tinged with anxiety as he spoke-in shock at seeing this man alive and well, and in every sense of the word, as if nothing ever happened to him-nothing scratched his face; breathing, functioning like a man who had never been through hell.

(A question that implies that Thomas had fallen into the clutches of Democrats during the civil war.)

Thomas began to murmur, "It wasn't eas- "

"ATTENTION WORKERS! YES, THE LOYAL AND MIGHTY WORKERS!" Thus blasted the sting of radio as it cut short into the sentence.

All gaze within the room immediately turn on to the radio without any second thought.

"THERE IS A MESSAGE FROM THE SUPREME LEADER HIMSELF:
THIS VICTORY OF OURS—YES, THE MIGHTY VICTORY—SHALL NEVER BE FORGOTTEN IN THE DUST OF HISTORY.
FREE, FREE, FREE BEER FOR EVERYONE, IN THE TOWN SQUARE AT 4 PM, AFTER THE INAUGURATION OF OUR SUPREME LEADER'S GLORIOUS MONUMENT."

The news of free beer quickly spread through the nation, as the speaking machines blared the announcement.

"We were in a beer crisis during the civil war, and now, all of a sudden, we have enough to give it away for free," Elias thought.

But then he caught himself. "No, the party is doing all this for our own good. I shouldn't doubt their intentions"

His thoughts crumbled under the relentless flood of party propaganda, seeping in every second from every direction.

Excitement rippled through the room, and the earlier conversations were instantly replaced with enthusiastic chatter about the free beer and fervent praise for the leader.

People cried out together, shouting, *"Workers rise, economy drive, country thrive,"* demonstrating how effectively the speaking machine has woven this philosophy into everyone's soul. The motto is now inseparable from the workers, just as the soul is to the body.

Suddenly, Comrade Franklin came running toward Elias and Thomas, breathless. "The secretary head wants to meet you, Elias. Personally."

IV
MANIFESTO

Elias apologized to Thomas and invited him to his home for dinner. Thomas responded with a slight grin on his face, *"No worries, I will certainly pay a visit and catch up with each other, Comrade Elias Vayne."*

Elias wondered, on his walk to the secretary head's office chamber, what could warrant such an intimate discussion. Was it something related to the party? Or perhaps just another routine spy assignment? *"I doubt any Democrat still exist after the civil war,"* he thought. Despite having participated in several missions and survived the entire civil war, his trembling hands betrayed him in the battle against restlessness.

He was curious about the new secretary head and what type of man he might be.

Elias knocked on the door three times. A gruff, cracking voice from the secretary beckoned him to come inside.

As Elias stepped into the dimly lit room, he could barely make out the secretary's face. The faint light highlighted deep wrinkles stretched across his skin and his whitish hair.

"Ah! The new secretary, perhaps in his 60s," Elias thought as he stood before him.

"Howdy, Mr., how can I aid ya?" said Elias with a forced smile on his face, trying to hide his shivering nerves.

"Mr? Mr, you say? Oh our dear fancy democrat Mr. Elias Vayne eh?"

Elias started fumbling, sweat breaking across his forehead. *"N...no...?"*

A speaking machine passed by, visible from the window just behind the secretary head. Its mechanical voice echoed faintly: *"Free, free, free beer..."*

"Enough!" screamed the secretary head. *"It's 'Comrade.' We are all equal. Have you forgotten the party's main motto? And you have the audacity to work for the party as a spy while acting like a Democrat?"*

"I had a serious job for you, Comrade Elias Vayne, but I think you need some party teachings before that."

The secretary head slammed a party manifesto onto Elias's face. *"Read it all by today and memorize it—engrave it in every cell of your worthless body. And this is your first and last warning, ELIAS."*

Elias fumblingly replied, *"I am deeply regre—"*

"BE GONE AT ONCE!" shouted the secretary head. "I don't want to hear any of it. Utter a single word, and I'll have you hanged in the town square during the inauguration of the statue."

V
BRAVO

Elias's heart was still pounding. His encounter with the secretary had not gone well, but he was used to it; the previous secretary had been no different from this old hag.

I call myself a loyal member of the NSPP, yet I'm still foolish enough to address the secretary as "Mister." Perhaps I truly need some "loyalist therapy," Elias sighed, recalling an article he'd read that morning in the newspaper delivered by the ever-reliable speaking machine.

His disappointment didn't linger for long. The announcement about free beer at the town square resurfaced in his thoughts. He glanced sharply at the clock in the upper-left corner of the office—it was almost 2 p.m.

The radio blared: *"ATTENTION, WORKERS! YES, THE LOYAL AND MIGHTY WORKERS!"*

As expected, the announcement commanded the room's attention.

THE PARTY IS PLEASED ANNOUNCE THAT EVERYONE WILL BE RELEASED AT 2 P.M. TODAY. EVERYONE ATTEND INAUGURATION CEREMONY OF THE GLORIOUS STATUE OUR SUPREME LEADER. AND

DON'T FORGET ABOUT THE FREE, FREE, FREE BEER!

"The workers rise, the economy drives, the country thrives," repeated the crowd in perfect unison, their enthusiasm electric.

No wonder the radio always makes a grammatical mistake or two... or maybe it's intentional? Elias wondered.

The workers cheered and prepared to leave. Tears rolled from the eyes of party members and citizens alike, their prayers whispered toward the statue yet to be unveiled. But deep down, everyone knew the true source of their excitement—the free beer.

Elias followed the crowd toward the town square. The path felt unfamiliar, altered by the scars of war.

"I never expected this many people to still be alive in this town after the war," Elias thought.

The streets were drenched in decoration. Party flags draped every surface, and flowers rained down upon the gathering crowd—a spectacle likely orchestrated by the newly formed Welfare Ministry.

At the square, Elias noticed more crowds filtering in from West Parserland. To his mild surprise, even some from the democrat-dominated South Parserland were present. *"We'd rather die protecting democracy than live under NSPP,"* he recalled the famous Southern quote.

All eyes turned to the statue, still veiled by the party flag.

"By my estimate, it must be around 200 meters tall. I've never seen such an enormous statue in my life," Elias murmured.

"Truly, it's unbelievable," replied a stranger beside him.

Did I said that loud? Elias wondered awkwardly.

Soldiers lined every building terrace, their eyes locked on the crowd below. Three speaking machines stood tall on the stage, flanking a podium where the General of Parserland stepped forward.

"QUIET!" shouted the General. His voice, though commanding, had an oddly pleasant timbre.

The murmurs stopped instantly. Even the soldiers shifted slightly, their focus sharpening.

The General cleared his throat and began:

"Comrades, we all know why we have gathered here today. I would like to thank our Supreme Leader, who led us to this glorious victory. Today, we inaugurate this mighty statue so that this day will forever be remembered, even by comrades in the farthest corners of Parserland. The world will bow before us. We, the citizens of Parserland, are the most dominant force on Earth. No power can crush us, and your loyalty to the party is deeply appreciated."

The General raised his arm.

"Repeat after me: THE WORKERS RISE, THE ECONOMY DRIVES, THE COUNTRY THRIVES!"

The crowd roared in unison, their voices so thunderous it felt as though the earth itself trembled.

Elias's gaze drifted to the concrete walls dividing Parserland into its four regions—North, South, East, and West. *What purpose do these walls serve?* he wondered.

The General's voice boomed again:

"AND THE TRAITORS MUST DIE, SHOULDN'T THEY?"

A cheer erupted from the crowd.

One hundred and ten prisoners from South Parserland were presented on stage, their heads covered with black cloth. The crowd roared with anticipation, hats flying into the air in a chaotic frenzy.

Caught in the excitement, Elias instinctively reached for his scalp, only to realize he wasn't wearing a hat.

"I'm so stupid," he sighed.

The General raised his hand once more.

"COUNT WITH ME!"

"THREE!" roared the crowd.

"TWO!"

The air was thick with anticipation.

'ONE!"

A lever was pulled by a man from North Parserland, his facial features distinct—narrow eyes, a smaller nose, and wild hair.

The execution was over in seconds.

At the same moment, the party flag draped over the statue fell away, revealing the colossal figure of the Supreme Leader in all its imposing glory.

Citizens from every direction roared. The crowd stood frozen, their faces awash with awe and fear, yet the statue offered a sense of protection at the same time.

Elias cheered alongside them, his voice blending into the sea of chants and slogans. But his eyes remained fixed, not on the grand statue, but on the speaking machines rolling through the crowd, their crates overflowing with free beer.

VI

LOST

Elias, after having consumed gallons of free beer and watching the exhausting inauguration of the mighty statue—larger than anything he had ever witnessed before—was walking through the hustle and bustle of the Central East Market of Parserland. The streetlamps were mostly flickering, as most of them had been installed decades ago, and these mere streetlights couldn't sustain the fumes of the civil war, perhaps. It was quite surprising to see winds blowing so strong at this hour in the month of June.

The city was blooming after the war, but soldiers still kept an eye on everyone passing by. The city was full of lights, which resembled the flag of the party, and the sellers shouted about their products. People barely bought things from the Central East Market, as the prices were sky-high—perhaps they'd reach the sun soon?

Elias soon took the quiet lane that connected to his house; he rarely opted for this path. The street was quiet and had no streetlamps, except for a few spaced every 300-400 meters. Elias took out his torch and thought about

Maria, his lost love in the civil war. He hadn't seen her since the war started. She was somewhat of a democrat supporter, but Elias had never uttered a single word against her.

"Ah, wish I could just have a mere sight of her. I write a letter every week and post it, without mentioning any address, because I don't know where you are, my love."

Soon, he reached the caller machine, which was installed on nearly every street. Elias never missed a day without calling the love of his life, probably lost in the treacherous wars of Parserland. He opened the gate; the old door made an unpleasant sound, but Elias was used to it.

Elias took out a letter Maria had given him four years ago before the civil war started, when she was sent on an annual health mission to help the dying soldiers in the hospital. Perhaps she never returned... The letter was more like a scrap of paper with a number on it—one Maria had asked Elias to call whenever he missed her.

Elias dialed:

5 5 6 4 5 6 0 4... The page had long been torn apart years ago , leaving the last digits lost to time. He could never reach her, but he still tried different numbers every day, hoping the caller machine would somehow send his message to her.

He added three more random sets of numbers which he had never tried before.

The caller machine began to ring, which was surprising to Elias. The machine always said the number didn't exist on any of the previous number sets he had entered. But this time, the call connected.

"Hello? Who is it?" a random woman asked curiously.

"Maria? Is it you?" Elias cried out.

"No, wrong number!" she replied, and the call disconnected.

Elias stood frozen in the booth, staring blankly at the machine. The weight of disappointment settled heavy in his chest.

Soon a sharp knock on the door startled him.

"Hello? Are you done, comrade? Let me in, I want to use the caller machine!" a stranger said anxiously.

Elias got up, shook his head, and left the booth with no reaction on his face, but Maria's image still circled in his mind. He dropped the letter he had written for Maria this week in the letterbox beside the caller machine.

"Maybe one day…" Elias sighed.

Walking down the street toward his home, the place was shrouded in darkness, with the faint light from his torch barely lighting a short distance ahead. Cold winds surrounded Elias Vyane. He began to hum a song that used to be Maria's personal favorite:

It's you and me,
Love me as if forever is ours.
Never let my hands drift away from yours,
As the moon revolves around the earth,
My world revolves around you.

Elias cried as he could not recall any more of the song. He feared losing any memory of her and longed to keep them all preserved within him.

Soon, he reached apartment 189, where he lived. The elevator was still under maintenance, as usual, so he took the stairs. Each step felt heavier than the last, his movements growing unsteady—probably the aftereffect of the beer overdose.

He pulled out his key and unlocked the old wooden door, pretending it was a sword plunging into the face of a democrat. The room was dark, and he didn't bother looking around. He simply stumbled to the bed and collapsed onto it. Within a second or two, he was fast asleep, like a bear in hibernation

VII

Puzzle or Pizzle

The clock struck and cried at four in the morning.

Work. Work! Work? Followed by the usual party motto.

Elias was still unconscious yet dizzy, his vision blurry. The aftereffects of the beer still hadn't left him.

A heavy thud startled Elias as it struck the balcony door. "Ah, must be the newspaper," he muttered.

He got up from his bed and cautiously opened the old wooden door. Bending down, he grabbed the newspaper, presumably tossed by the speaking machine. Below, kids were chasing after it, waving their hands excitedly.

But it wasn't the scene below that captivated Elias. It was the sky above—something he had never seen before. An enormous zeppelin, 420 feet long and 38 feet in diameter, flew nearly 500 meters away, tearing through the clouds. Its cylindrical frame, internal gas cells, and roaring engines made it an imposing sight.

At the bottom of the zeppelin, a banner painted in national colors hung proudly, the party's motto written across it in bold letters, visible even to the farthest corners of the town.

"Wait, there's some kind of flyer being dropped in masses for the people of Parserland. Is it some new announcement? Perhaps free beer? Free rations?"

Elias wasted no time. Grabbing his office coat—which he didn't bother wearing but draped over his shoulders—and stuffing a piece of bread into his mouth, he rushed outside.

Ignoring the fixed lift, which had been repaired while he was snoring the night away, Elias took the stairs two at a time. His eyes remained locked on the zeppelin above, forgetting even the rubble-strewn streets.

"What a magnificent beauty it is!" he whispered in awe.But fate had other plans. His left foot caught in a pile of debris, sending him sprawling onto the dirt. Undeterred, he stuffed the fallen piece of bread back into his mouth and continued running.

Out of breath, Elias finally joined a growing crowd of adults, teenagers, and children, all trying to catch the falling flyers. People pushed and shoved, desperate to grab one.

Elias noticed a man stumble over a piece of rubble, only to be trampled by the oblivious crowd. The horrifying scene froze Elias for a brief moment, but he knew stopping to help would mean being crushed underfoot himself.

The zeppelin loomed directly overhead, casting its massive shadow across the crowd. Flyers rained down like an aristocrat tossing coins at desperate serfs.

Elias leaped and snatched one from the air. The once-cheering crowd fell silent as eyes scanned the bold letters on the paper.

WAR. WAR. WAR.
COMRADES,   UNITE TOGETHER. THE COUNTRY CALLS. YOUR FAITH IN THE LEADER AND SUPPORT

FROM THE WORKERS WILL LEAD US TO ANOTHER VICTORY.

The weight of the announcement settled heavily on Elias's chest.

The silence shattered as the crowd erupted into chants of the party motto. Elias sighed heavily, his voice trembling as he whispered, "Another war. Another destruction. And the loop continues."

The crowd's reaction, though predictable, still unsettled him. They chanted with blind fervor:

"The leader we trust knows what's best! Bravo! Yes, workers, rise up! The leader will lead us to another—another victory!"

The flyer slipped from Elias's trembling hands, carried away by the wind. Yet, he forced himself to march alongside the others. His steps blended into the collective rhythm, his voice joining the chants—not out of loyalty, but because the collective roar gave him a fleeting sense of security.

Elias walked in a daze, unaware of where his feet carried him, until the crowd passed his office building.

"This is destiny. And destiny is this," he whispered to himself.

Pushing through the crowd, Elias stepped into the office building. Thomas was waiting at the reception floor.

"Hey, Elias!" Thomas called out.

But Elias, still trapped in the fog of his trauma, walked past him without a word. Thomas jogged ahead, blocking his path.

"I'm so sorry, Elias! I drank too much last night and couldn't make it to dinner. Anyways, secretary has called you again."

Unfazed, Elias brushed past Thomas, shoulders colliding.

"What's he up to?" Thomas sighed.

Elias barely registered Thomas's words as he walked toward the secretary's chamber.

"Ah! The manifesto! I forgot to read it!" Anxiety gripped Elias as he knocked three times on the door—the secret code for rank identification.

"Enter," said the secretary.

Elias stepped inside, his face pale.

"Listen, Elias. I hope you've read the manifesto?"

"Y-Yes... I did," Elias stammered.

"Good. Now listen carefully. You're aware of the war announcement made by the mighty Zeppelin, correct?"

Elias nodded.

"Your task won't be easy, comrade. The party is counting on you. Your job is to eavesdrop on individuals conspiring against us in South Parserland. Report every detail—names, addresses. What happens to them afterward is none of your concern."

Elias rolled his eyes internally. "I wasn't going to ask anyway."

"Consider it done, comrade," he said aloud, his chest swelling with newfound determination.

"Ah, that's what I like to hear, comrade. Now go. Report back as soon as you have information."

Elias left before the secretary could change his mind.

The bell rang, and Radio Channel 7 crackled to life: *"It's time for lunch. Please proceed to Canteen 89 for today's meal."*

Elias joined Thomas for lunch. Soup and bread again. The soup looked like murky sewage water, and the smell turned his stomach. But with no alternatives, he forced it down.

"Are you okay, comrade? I'm really sorry for missing dinner last night," Thomas said firmly.

"Oh? Don't worry about it, mate. Everyone was drunk last night. I'm fine," Elias replied.

"If you say so. But tonight, I'll definitely visit," Thomas said with a smile.

The radio channels switched back to war announcements. The crowd cheered once again. Even Thomas joined in.

Elias hesitated, fear flickering in his eyes. But when Thomas noticed his silence, Elias awkwardly raised his hand and began chanting the party motto.

The loop continues.

VIII

We Hear You

"I have to leave, Comrade Thomas," said Elias hurriedly.

"Yeah? But where are you going?" asked Thomas.

"I don't have time to explain at the moment; it's party work," replied Elias and dashed off without wasting another second.

"Ah! This guy..." sighed Thomas, but his attention was soon caught by the sight of Misty.

Elias checked the time—it was already 12:30 PM, and the last metro to South Parserland for the day would leave at 12:40 PM.

He rushed to catch the train, running as fast as he could, pushing through crowds and shielding himself from scattered rubble.

While passing through the Central East Market, the usual hustle and bustle and the melodic chants of the sellers slowed him down. The metro station lay just beyond the market.

"Suddenly, a mob grabbed Elias by the arm, stopping him out of suspicion, assuming he was a thief. 'Show me your ID and state your purpose, or I'll throw you into the labor camp where the Democrats would love to have an extra pair of hands!'

Elias pleaded with tears rolling down his eyes, *"O mighty officer, please let me go! I have urgent tidings to settle. The entire Parserland depends on me at this moment!"*

The mob burst into laughter. *"What rubbish! And I am the supreme leader himself, kid"*

However, amused by the way Elias addressed him as a mighty officer, the man let him go.

"I'm such a great actor," Elias praised himself as he sprinted toward the station. But when he checked the time, it was already 12:45 PM.

Disappointment washed over him. "I'm going to lose this job. Why am I so stupid? Goddamn it! Just for the sake of lunch, I missed this too!" he cursed under his breath.

"Attention, workers!" blared the train committee speaker. "The train to South Parserland is delayed by 10 minutes. We apologize for the inconvenience."

Elias froze for a moment before joy lit up his face. Overwhelmed with relief, he gasped, "Thank you so much, God. I can't thank you enough!"

A few minutes later, Elias managed to secure a seat on the crowded train. The carriage was packed, mostly due to the recent war announcement. Many people from South Parserland had been working in Central East Parserland and were given a day to leave the region. Meanwhile, the citizens of Central East Parserland were urged not to harm anyone today, as maintaining war discipline was crucial for the party to showcase the NSPP regime's order and control over the enemy territories.

Soon, a woman around Elias's age with Southern features approached him. She had brown eyes, fair skin with a slight brown undertone, and long black hair.

"From the South?" she asked curiously.

Elias fumbled, taken aback by her beauty. It had been a year since he'd had a real conversation with a woman after Maria's disappearance.

"N-No," he stammered.

The woman eyed him with suspicion, seemingly wondering if he worked for the party.

Elias quickly realized he couldn't reveal his true identity.

"Yes, I'm from the South," he replied, lying smoothly. "I'm going to visit my sick grandmother. Can't leave her there in such a war-torn area, right?"

"True indeed," the woman responded. "I'm on my way to visit my parents too, and thinking of settling down in the South."

Then, lowering her voice, she whispered in Elias's ear, "I don't feel comfortable with the NSPP regime."

A twinge of anger sparked in Elias. As he still supported the NSPP, and was working for them, but he quickly masked his feelings. She was his lead, after all.

"I see," Elias replied, forcing a grin. "I've been thinking about joining the democrats myself. I don't like the ideology of the NSPP at all." He widened his eyes and smirked, playing the part convincingly. Years of espionage had made him an expert in controlling his expressions.

"What's your name, Mr. Democrat?" she asked, her smile widening.

"Elias," he said. *"And you , Mrs. Democrat?"*

"Sofia," she replied firmly.

"My father works for the Democrats, in a very prominent position with the United Democratic Party of Parserland," Sofia continued. "Why don't you join us for dinner? Several other Democrats will be there. We'd be pleased to have you and your grandmother if you can make it." She scribbled down her address on a piece of paper and handed it to him

Why not? Just consider me there!" replied Elias confidently.

"With your grandmother, right? She must have a wealth of knowledge and experience about the war. Her insights could really help us build a strategy," Sofia said eagerly.

"Ah, yes... w-with my grandmother," Elias stammered, trying to keep his composure , here was an awkward silence between them, lingering and heavy.

Suddenly, a stranger approached—a man with sharp brown eyes, slightly dark-toned skin, and neatly combed black hair. He wore an expensive suit, perfectly tailored, and carried an air of authority.

"I believe you've made a mistake, madam. This is my seat, isn't it?" the stranger said politely but firmly.

"Is it? Let me check my ticket," Sofia replied, fumbling slightly as she pulled it out.

"Ah, see—68," she continued, holding up the ticket.

The stranger leaned in slightly, his expression amused. *"Ma'am, you're holding it upside down. It's actually 89,"* he said, gently flipping the ticket in her hand.

Embarrassed, Sofia's cheeks flushed pink as she stammered an apology. *"Oh... I'm so sorry!"*

She quickly stood up, clutching her belongings, and proceeded towards the correct coach.

Elias had been silently observing the exchange, his face devoid of any expression. But beneath the calm exterior, a storm of regret brewed.

I should've asked her more questions—about her father, his role, his connections. What exactly did he do for the Democrats? Or perhaps pressed her for details about the democrat

conspiracy against the NSPP. I let a golden opportunity slip through my fingers.

His thoughts lingered on the encounter as the stranger settled into the now-empty seat. The brief conversation replayed in his mind over and over again, each word dissected, each pause analyzed, as if he could somehow extract more meaning from it.

Perhaps the myths were true after all. The Southerners really aren't very educated, he muttered under his breath, though the words felt hollow.

The conversation was long over, yet the weight of missed opportunities clung to him, a silent companion that stayed by his side for the rest of the journey to the South.

IX

Pair of Eyes

It was 7 PM. Elias finally stepped off the train in South Parserland, and the sight before him left him momentarily frozen. The station was in a miserable condition, as if it had been waiting for renovation for decades. The place had a foul smell of urine, which lingered in the air. Rations had already been cut for the southern region since the start of the civil war.

Beggars were in a depressed state, their faces devoid of any hope. Posters of many political leaders were plastered all over the station, asking for votes for the next general election of South Parserland. Almost everyone had a small pocket radio, which was constantly announcing the same message about the war being declared against them. A teenager came running towards Elias.

"Here, take this, mister! The South will never give up!" smiled the young man. His face was covered with dirt, and his hat was in miserable condition, with typical Southerner facial features.

It was a small poster on which it was written:

"We'd rather die protecting democracy than live under NSPP. Join us. We need you! For the war, for the Southerners. We shall never surrender."

And the address was the same as the one Sofia had scribbled.

"They are trying so hard," sighed Elias.

He knew deep down that the Southerners had no chance against the NSPP, who possessed advanced weapons, massive tanks, and mighty zeppelins.

"How are these democrats still so hopeful about the war? They are living in such poor conditions. How will they even sustain another war? What is so special in their ideology that ties them together?" Elias questioned to himself.

Just beside the train station was a market. He was surprised to see that there were no streetlights in the area, or if there were, none really worked.

With tons of questions running through his mind, he walked toward Sofia's house with the hope of catching up with his lead. Everyone was holding an old-fashioned lamp, and the market was dimly lit. Elias felt as though he had traveled back in time.

As he passed through the market, vendors shouted about their goods' prices with melodic songs they had created about their products. However, the peace did not last long. Soon, a fight erupted between a fruit vendor and a shabby democrat with scratches all over his face, as he couldn't afford bread anymore.

"Hand me those loaves of bread! Don't you hear? My family will starve because of you! How dare you raise the price of bread?" screamed the shabby democrat, holding the vendor's collar. However, if anyone had looked closely, they would have noticed the tears rolling down his face. There was nothing he could do to save his family. The faces of his kids must have been haunting him at that very moment.

"Th-there is nothing I can do, mister. The price of bread is skyrocketing these days. I'm barely selling them at a loss," stammered the vendor, fear clearly visible on his face.

But soon, people intervened and stopped the fight before the army could step in and worsen the situation. Elias sighed, his face reflecting pity. I fear what their condition will be by tomorrow when the NSPP launches a full-scale war, he thought, continuing his search for the address on the paper.

As he walked, Elias noticed a speaking machine slowly wandering through the area.

They have these here too? I wonder what they even use them for. Their voices were far quieter here, and this variant looked so old.

It was easy to distinguish between the old and new models. The older ones required a driver, while the newer versions were fully automatic and roamed freely through cities.

The machine approached Elias as they shared the same narrow lane, bound to exit the same way he had entered. Now close enough, Elias could hear its message clearly:

"Vote for your favorite and most loved Master Kafka!
Vote to throw off the NSPP from Parserland!
Vote for lower prices!
Vote for Master Kafka—political symbol: hat, number: 3rd!"

"Oh, they use it for political advertisements here? Elias thought. I think I'm lost. Should I ask the driver for directions? Wait... what if he catches my Northern accent?"

But then he reassured himself. Accents aren't as easily recognizable anymore. Many Southerners have worked in North Parserland, so speech patterns have blended together.

He waited for the speaking machine to stop nearby and then knocked on its window.

The driver rolled it down. He was an elderly man with wrinkles etched deep into his face, a black mustache—clearly dyed recently—and sharp Southern features. He wore a hat, the unmistakable mark of a Southern democrat.

"Hello, comrade? I'm lost. Do you know the way to this address?" Elias asked cautiously.

The driver's brows furrowed slightly. "Comrade?" he said with suspicion.

Elias quickly composed himself, forcing a smile. "Ah, silly me! I've been in North Parserland for a decade. It must've slipped out by habit."

The driver's face softened. "Oh? Then you must know a lot about the NSPP. Have you returned to help us?" he asked, hope flickering in his tired eyes

"Y-Yes, sir. I've come to serve my beloved South," "Could you please point me in the right direction? I seem to have lost my way."   Elias said with a confident smirk.

"Show me." The driver took the paper with a sense of pride, his chest puffed slightly as he realized he was helping someone who had supposedly returned from the North to aid their cause. "Ah! That's Sofia's house. A wonderful young lady! I've heard they're starting some sort of rebellion group to overthrow the NSPP."

Elias's eyes widened, his heart racing with excitement." I'm so close. I can't let this lead slip away "

"This house is right beside mine! If you don't mind, I can drop you off there. I'm heading home anyway," the driver offered with a warm smile.

Amazed by this unexpected hospitality—something he hadn't experienced in years—Elias agreed without any hesitation

It was his first time sitting inside a speaking machine.

"What is your name, mister?" asked the driver politely.

"Elias," he replied.

The driver scanned Elias from bottom to top, observing him as if he wanted to convey something but was holding back. Elias felt a bit uncomfortable under the driver's intense gaze and the awkward silence that filled the machine.

"And you, mister?" Elias asked, breaking the silence.

"F-Fistros, E-Elias Vyane," stammered the driver, his dull, old eyes widening as tears filled them.

"Wait... how do you know my full name?" Elias asked. Hearing his full name frightened him. He was scared the driver knew that he worked for the party. Also, he had never been to the South, as long as he could remember.

"I knew it! I recognize you from somewhere. You resemble someone I already knew," Fistros said with a hearty laugh.

"I knew your father's friend, Mr. Elias Vyane. Perhaps you were too small back then; how could you even remember?"

"M-my father?" Elias fumbled, his mind racing. All the flashbacks of the civil war played in front of him. The trauma he had buried began clawing its way to the surface.

"How is he? Is he here in the South by now? Because today was the last train, wasn't it? Elias?" Fistros asked.

Tears began to roll down Elias's cheeks. He couldn't utter a single word. He was frozen in place, staring at Fistros.

"Is he okay?" Fistros pressed gently.

"N-no... he—he fought bravely in the civil war, but..." Elias was shrouded in silence, pain visible in every word. His chest felt heavy, and his eyes spoke of the suffering he had endured from the civil war.

"Oh dear, I am so sorry," said Fistros sympathetically and held Elias's hands, offering a sense of comfort.

"It's getting late; we should get going," said the driver in a comforting manner.

Inserting keys into the speaking machine, the machine trembled with a roaring old engine sound mixed with the political announcement being played.

To distract himself, Elias started peeking outside the window of the machine, analyzing the buildings and trying to remember the streets—a task made difficult by the darkness, despite being in the city center. Only the faint glow of lamps, visible in the hands of people, provided minimal light.

Soon, a brown male dog, covered all over with hair and with eyes barely visible, appeared, running beside the speaking machine.

"He clearly looks like someone's pet, who lacks care—or maybe his owner most likely abandoned him", thought Elias while waving at the dog

"His name is Jai. People say his owner imported this dog from South Asia. He wanders here in the market itself. It's strange to see him in this lane today. However, his owner abandoned him when prices rose unexpectedly, and they were no longer able to feed him," said Fistros.

"Oh? Is that it? They just abandoned the dog like that?" Disappointed, Elias looked at the dog again and searched his pocket to see if he had something to feed Jai.

"Ah! I might have a breadcrumb in my pocket. Here it is!" Elias s with enthusiasm.

He tossed the breadcrumb at Jai, shouting, "Here, comrade! Have a good night's dinner."

Fistros looked at Elias with suspicion and scolded, "You should start practicing the word 'mister' or else some army man will catch you without even listening to your explanation, understood?"

Elias nodded his head.

After traveling for half an hour through South Parserland, Elias felt like a time traveler, observing scenes that reminded him of decades-old sights from the North. He was jotting down everything he found unusual about the South in his small diary.

"You like writing as well? I used to do a lot when I was your age! Nowadays, people here barely get access to education due to the constant wars" said Fistros with a sigh.

"Here we are! That old building with the renovated windows—that's where Sofia lives. Shall I drop you here?" asked Fistros.

"Y-yes, mister," Elias fumbled, feeling nervous about his plan.

Fistros stopped the speaking machine near Sofia's house and invited Elias to visit his home someday. "It's just two houses north of Sofia's."

"Certainly!" smiled Elias.

Sofia's house was adorned with lights. However, it still looked old, and a banner was tied to the door with something written in a strange language. Elias walked a few steps closer to have a better look.

Is this Old Parser language? People barely use it anymore, neither in the North nor the South. I might have an Old Parser translator dictionary in my bag."

Elias pulled the dictionary out while keeping his eyes fixed on the poster.

"FREEDOMEAS... This might translate to 'freedom,' I suppose," Elias murmured, flipping through the pages of the dictionary to confirm the word.

Suddenly, the door creaked open, startling Elias.

"Who is it? Oh, Elias! What are you doing standing outside? Come in, we've been waiting for you!" said Sofia.

"So-Sofia?" Elias stammered, a shy grin spreading across his face.

"Come, follow me," Sofia said with a warm smile.

Elias followed her inside the house

"your grandmother? How is she? I can't see her with you?" asked Sofia

"She couldn't make it. When I informed her about this meeting, she instead pleaded with me, saying she wanted to rest for a while," Elias lied smoothly.

X
Freedom

As Elias entered the house, his eyes searched each and every corner. The interior was just as miserable as it appeared from the outside. Mice ran across the floor, and wherever he looked, he was surprised by how clean yet old ,everything felt begging desperately for renovation. The house lacked any color. If I had to put it simply, I'd say it looked grey and cold at the same time.

As Elias stepped into a shabby-looking room, he noticed tens, maybe even hundreds, of people gathered there. It was obvious they were all democrats.

Sofia asked Elias to wait in the room while she hurried towards what could barely be called a stage—it was more like a table with a microphone attached to it. The room was decorated with democrat flags, featuring blue, red, and green stripes. In the middle of the flag, the word "FREEDOMEAS" was written, meaning freedom in Old Parser.

Do these colors represent something? Elias wondered. Like the NSPP's flag?

"Attention, attention!" Sofia called out, clearing her throat while forcing a small smile.

She looked nervous, yet there was boldness in her stance.

"We've all gathered here to discuss the sudden announcement of war by those bloody goatfuckers—the NSPP. Didn't they have enough joy destroying us in the civil war? But this time, gentlemen and women, we will not hold back. We will fight till we die, till our last breath—for our beloved country, for our ideology, for our families!"

A fellow democrat suddenly stood up in the middle of her speech. Tears streamed down his face as he spoke, his voice trembling and weak.

"W-we should surrender... Al-already our prices are skyrocketing. We barely have anything to eat at home. Our families are dying of starvation, ma'am. We cannot hold on any longer."

The man sat back down, his shoulders trembling as he wept aloud. His words seemed to drain the energy from the room, and the morale of everyone present sank.

One more person stood up and said, "Democracy creates inequality between the rich and poor anyway. Why should we even support this country?"

The room erupted into loud cheers and shouts directly aiming Sofia.

Elias watched, stunned. How could people turn against each other so quickly? The air was filled with hostility, and everyone seemed to be criticizing one another

Raising her hand, Sofia addressed the crowd, "Ah! It seems many of you have been swayed by the flyers dropped by the NSPP zeppelins over South Parserland. They said things like, 'Democracy means you'll be poor, and I'll be rich.' Clever propaganda, isn't it? But let me tell you what democracy truly represents—freedom. Freedom to speak, freedom to criticize, just like you are all doing right now. Under NSPP rule, none of this would be possible. You'd be dead for even trying."

Elias found himself nodding slightly. "She's not wrong... Wait, why am I agreeing? What am I thinking? Silly me!"

Sofia's voice grew more forceful. "Freedom to vote, everyone. Once the NSPP takes control, voting will disappear. You won't have the right to speak against their supreme leader. Your choices, your body—nothing will belong to you anymore. They will own it all. Those so-called 'comrades' preach equality, but look closer. Their leaders hoard wealth while their people suffer in silence."

"Remember the free beer distribution up north? Many of us went there. Did you see their faces? The hunger, the desperation—they weren't faces of equality. And now those same people want to invade our fertile, beloved South Parserland and drag us into their misery."

She slammed her hand down on the table, her voice so sharp.

"So tell me, will we kneel and hand over everything we have? Or will we rise—rise with whatever weapons we can find, with whatever strength we have left? I'd rather die fighting for democracy than live under their tyranny."

Her words hung in the air unshakable. Murmurs of agreement spread through the crowd as her message sank in.

Elias thought to himself, "That almost convinced me. But still... they don't stand a chance against our leader. These grand speeches sound powerful, but are they real? Or just tools to persuade these desperate southerners against the NSPP?

XI

BLIND PATRIOT

The speech lasted an hour, followed by discussions and debates. Elias sat silently, trying to remember everything said so he could later inform the Secretary.

"Ladies and gentlemen, with this note, I would like to end my speech.

LONG LIVE THE PARSERS!"

The air in the room was thick with the roar of the crowd. Anger and revenge ran through their veins.

"I wonder what will happen if they ever find out I work for the party," Elias thought, rolling his eyes with a sigh.

Sofia stepped off the stage, immediately surrounded by people praising her speech. However, she managed to push through the crowd and rushed toward Elias.

"Is she coming towards me?" Elias wondered.

"How was it?" Sofia asked, tiredly trying to catch her breath.

"It was good" gruffly replied elias and walked out of the room.

He knew he would betray her sooner or later and didn't want to risk forming any kind of feelings toward her.

Sofia stood still there for a moment with disappointment crossing her face. But soon, two other men surrounded her, praising her knowledge and beauty, pulling her attention away from Elias.

Elias walked down the narrow streets of South Parserland, thousands of thoughts wandering through his head—and perhaps also any place to sleep. All the nearby hotels had already closed early because of the war announcement. Suddenly, his mind snapped, and he remembered that Fistros' house was just two doors north of Sofia's.

As he made his way to Fistros' house, he noticed Jai following him.

Elias sat down on a bench. "Hey, mister democrat dog, you look cute, but sorry, I don't have any more breadcrumbs," Elias said with a hearty laugh and patted Jai.

Jai clearly enjoyed Elias's company; it was evident in how comfortable he seemed around him.

Elias finally reached Fistros' house and knocked on the door.

"Hello? Is anybody here? It's me, Elias," he called out.

Soon, the door opened, and Fistros' wife stood there.

"Who are you, young man? What brings you here at this hour?" she asked.

"I'm so sorry to disturb you at this hour, ma'am. Is Fistros here? I'd like to have a word or two with him."

Fistros was already approaching the door; as the voice sounded familiar.

"Hey, it's Elias! Come in kid, come in," he said with a warm welcome that overwhelmed Elias.

The house felt oddly familiar, almost like Sofia's. Maybe all Southern houses followed a similar design.

They all sat in the living room—Mr. and Mrs. Fistros on one side of the sofa, and Elias on the other.

"So, tell me, what happened, Elias?" Mr. Fistros asked with weary eyes.

"It's... well, sir, my wallet got stolen as soon as I stepped out of Sofia's house after the meeting. And my wallet had the keys to my home. Please, sir, do me a favor—I need a place to stay for the night. I can pay you as well," Elias said, faking tears as he pulled out his wallet. Deep down, he knew they would refuse any payment.

"N-No, son, we don't want any kind of money. This is your home too. You can stay here as long as you need; no need to worry about anything," Mr. Fistros said warmly.

"No need to worry about anything at all," Mrs. Fistros added with a gentle smile.

"Thank you so much. I can't describe how much you both have helped me. I'll forever be in your debt," Elias said, tears rolling down his face.

"Show him the room on the second floor," Mr. Fistros said, turning to his wife.

"Come, follow me, lad," she said softly, gesturing for Elias to follow her upstairs

Elias stood up and followed her upstairs. He felt relieved knowing he wouldn't have to spend the night on the streets.

Mrs. Fistros opened the door to a modest room. "This used to be our son's room," she said softly.

"Where is he now? In the North?" Elias asked out of curiosity.

Mrs. Fistros fumbled with her words before breaking into quiet sobs. "H-He was martyred... fighting bravely in the civil war, protecting our beloved South."

"I'm so sorry for your loss. I understand... I lost my parents in the war too," Elias replied, a faint smile trembling on his lips as tears welled in his eyes. He stepped forward and hugged Mrs. Fistros in an attempt to comfort her.

The room was primarily wooden, filled with the scent of age yet maintained with evident care. Military medals hung on the wall to the left of the door, glinting under the dim light. A portrait of Fistros' son rested proudly on a side table, and a large South Parserland flag hung on the wall, its presence both somber and magnificent. In one corner, an old Enfield rifle leaned against the wall, a silent witness to the past.

Elias sat on the bed and pulled out his *Secwrite*—a compact typing machine capable of sending letters directly to the Secretary of an individual's department without the need for a post office. Responses typically arrived the following day.

With a deep sigh, Elias began typing. He reported his observations, detailed the tense atmosphere in South Parserland, and recounted Sofia's speech, which had stirred rebellion-like energy among the townsfolk.

Once satisfied, Elias sent the letter to his Secretary and set the *Secwrite* aside.

What an irony, right? Sitting in a room that belonged to a patriot of the South, and yet here I am, doing the complete opposite in the same room."

Elias, unable to sleep, grew bored and decided to explore the room a bit more.

He walked over to the desk and started searching through it. Soon, he found a diary tucked away in one of the drawers.

"This might contain information useful to me," Elias said firmly.

He opened the book from the last page, assuming that people often wrote important things towards the end.

It turned out to be the journal of Fistros' son, where he had documented his days almost daily. The final entry was dated the day before he died:

If someone is ever reading this diary, then I am probably dead by now.

The civil war feels like it's coming to an end.

We can no longer hold our position; we are outnumbered.

Anytime now, they will reach our trench and start the butchering.

But we still haven't lost our faith.

We are going to fight one last time, with our full strength.

Here I go—to save my motherland, for you.

Thank you, my beloved land, for providing me with everything I could ever ask for.

Long live the South.

Elias stared at the page, the weight of the words sinking into him.

He closed the diary gently and placed it back where he found it and laid down on bed. The silence of the room hung heavy around him.

The sound of a distant bomb woke him up.

"What was that?" thought Elias as he instantly checked the time. It was midnight—sharp 12 a.m.

"It's 12 a.m.," Elias muttered, terrified. "NSPP has launched a full-scale war in the South now."

He grabbed his Secwrite and checked for any response from the secretary head. The Secwrite began printing a message:

"Inform us of the meeting area location, Elias.
We shall blow away the site and the neighboring areas. They
shall fear the strength of NSPP. Report as soon as you read this."

Soon, the sirens blared to alert people about the war. The noise of aircraft engines was audible even inside the room. It sounded like hundreds of planes were flying overhead, sending a shiver down Elias's spine.

Without wasting a second, Elias grabbed his belongings from the room along with the old rusty rifle and bullets, just in case of an emergency.

He rushed out of the house without informing Mr. Fistros. However, he saw him running with the rifle. He tried to call out, but too old to chase him.

The city was ablaze, bombs dropped by the NSPP reducing it to ashes. Screams filled the air—people crying in pain, mourning the death of their loved ones. The sight was haunting.

Paratroopers from the NSPP aircraft descended from the sky. The once-dark night had turned into a fiery orange as the flames engulfed the city. Thick smoke rose into the heavens, swallowing the stars.

The devastation terrified Elias. It reminded him of the horrors he had witnessed during the years of civil war.

Running a few miles, Elias witnessed a civilian being mercilessly butchered by an NSPP soldier right in front of his eyes. Suddenly, a soldier shouted and charged toward Elias, aiming to stab him with his bayonet.

Elias screamed "Do-Don't , stay there! , I work for the party"

He managed to pull out his ID just in time, showing the soldier that he worked for the party. This convinced the soldier to lower his weapon and spare him.

Elias took a long breath to calm himself, his mind racing as he tried to figure out his next move to escape the chaos engulfing the city.

He ran in the north direction, hoping to reach the northern border of South Parserland.

The air was filled with the terrible sounds of bombs exploding and people screaming, with the horrifying sight of butchering happening right before his eyes. Overwhelmed, he darted into an abandoned house and hid in the corner of a room.

Memories of his father being butchered in front of him during the civil war surged back, paralyzing him with fear.

Suddenly, someone placed a hand on Elias' shoulder from behind, startling him.

"Elias? Is it you?" a familiar voice asked.

Too terrified to turn around, Elias screamed, "Don't kill me! Don't kill me!"

"It's me, Sofia," she said with a reassuring smile.

Elias hesitated before finally turning back, tears streaming down his face.

"Let's get out of here," Elias urged, his voice trembling.

"No," Sofia said firmly. "We have to protect our land. I see you already have a rifle. Come, let's go back home and decide what to do next. Some more rebels are joining us there."

Before Elias could respond, the Secwrite in his bag came alive, its mechanical voice whirring as it began printing updates.

Elias froze, his body drenched in sweat. He knew this was the moment—his identity would be exposed.

"What's that?" Sofia asked curiously, stepping closer.

The *Secwrite* finished printing:

"Thank you, Elias, for letting us know the location of the meeting area.
It is destroyed in fragments. Keep reporting to us. You are making your nation proud and will be rewarded suitably."

Elias' eyes widened in horror as he turned to look at Sofia.

Sofia stood motionless, her face pale with shock. The realization of betrayal hit her like a storm.

"They... they must all be dead..." Sofia whispered, her voice breaking as tears filled her eyes.

Without muttering a single word, Sofia walked away.

Elias stayed rooted to the spot, blaming himself for everything.

"I shouldn't have accepted this job in the first place. B-but... the NSPP is my everything. I have no family, no close ones." His voice trembled with regret as he stood up, deciding to follow Sofia and apologize to her.

The room was dark. Elias could barely see anything except the faint outline of the door. The echo of gunfire and the agonized screams of people outside reverberated through the walls, sending chills down his spine.

When he stepped outside, he caught a glimpse of Sofia. The entire neighborhood was ablaze, her black hair flying in the wind, her face dimly illuminated by the raging flames around her.

"Sofia!" Elias screamed her name at the top of his lungs.

Sofia turned back, her face streaked with tears, clearly visible even in the dim light.

Suddenly, a gunshot rang out.

The bullet struck Sofia's chest. Her expression froze, and her body crumpled lifelessly onto the street like a puppet with its strings cut.

Elias was horrified. He dropped to the ground, screaming uncontrollably.

In the distance, the mocking laughter of two Parserland soldiers echoed.

"That was a nice shot, comrade," one of them said.

"Wait... is that Elias Vayne? The one working in the spy department?" the other soldier asked, narrowing his eyes and approaching him.

The soldiers ran toward Elias, but he remained frozen, too traumatized to move.

"Get up, Elias. You're Elias, right?" one soldier asked, standing over him.

Elias stammered, barely audible, "Y-yes..." His face was a mask of fear, the horrors of war etched into his trembling features.

XII
North

The soldiers loaded Elias onto a truck and sent him to the North.

On the way, he drifted into a vision—a haunting memory.

He was walking alone in the bitter winter of the northernmost part of Parserland. It was ten years ago, in the midst of the civil war.

The landscape was blanketed with snow, and all around him were graves. Endless graves.

In front of him stood six crosses—Christian crosses—marking the resting places of his dearest friends.

Elias muttered under his breath, "Wish you were all here, comrades..."

A single tear rolled down his cheek, only to be carried away by the fierce snowstorm. Shivering badly, he pressed on.

He dragged through the snow, each step slow and cautious, mindful of the possibility of hidden bombs beneath the surface.

Eventually, exhaustion overtook him. The snowstorm had calmed, so he decided to ignite a bonfire.

After multiple failed attempts, he succeeded at last.

Reaching into his bag, he pulled out the last can of food he had. He ate it slowly, each bite accompanied by a flood of thoughts—memories of his comrades, regrets, and the unrelenting weight of survival.

Wishing he would never have to face the morning again.

A sudden jolt of the truck snapped Elias back to his senses. He was drenched in sweat yet shivering uncontrollably. However, being surrounded by North Parserland soldiers brought an unexpected sense of safety.

It had been another of his civil war nightmares, the kind that had plagued him for years.

"Hey? Where am I? Where are you taking me? I work for the party—don't you dare come any closer!" shouted Elias.

"Calm down, comrade. We're just taking you back to North Parserland," one of the soldiers replied with a smile.

The roads were completely destroyed, but the driver seemed to know a way through. Occasionally, the rubble of collapsed houses obstructed their path, forcing everyone to get out of the truck to clear the debris.

"So, what were you doing in the South? Spying as usual, eh?" one soldier asked.

Elias hesitated, staring at the soldier for a moment. "Usual spy work, of course. I don't have a passion for strolling into a deathbed," he replied with a yawn.

"Got anything to eat? I feel quite hungry," Elias added.

The soldier searched through his pocket and pulled out a piece of chocolate.

"Uh, here. I don't have much else, but ration supplies will rise soon—it was announced by the speaking machine itself. All glory to NSPP!"

The other soldiers echoed the chant with enthusiasm.

Awkwardly, Elias joined in, forcing himself to repeat the words to avoid drawing any suspicion.

The soldier then tossed the piece of chocolate to Elias, who ate it as if he hadn't eaten in ages.

"Nothing more?" Elias shouted.

"I'm afraid not," one of the soldiers replied.

Soon, they reached a war-torn area. The soldiers climbed out of the truck and instructed Elias to stay inside.

"This truck will take you back to North Parserland. We've already informed the driver," one soldier said.

The soldiers marched away, singing a famous NSPP marching song in unison:

We march, march, march along the road...
We fight for the land we love, yes, the beloved land of yours...
March for your supreme leader who is building a great nation for you...
March, my comrades, come together!
Fight, fight, fight! March, march, march!

Elias sighed as the truck proceeded northward.

The Secwrite began printing a new message, its rhythmic clattering filling the cabin and giving Elias a wave of nostalgia.

Elias, as soon as you reach the North, visit the secretary's office. He might reward you for your bravery, I suppose. — Thomas

"Ah, at last, something good awaits me? But perhaps I don't want to be rewarded by the hands of murderers," Elias thought. "Still, there's nothing I can do. The NSPP is everything for me right now. I can't escape its grasp or the loop it has trapped me in. It's almost impossible to express how I feel. This is my destiny. To survive, I must stick to the party—no matter what."

Elias peeked outside through the narrow truck window to figure out where he was. The cold air seeping in through the window carried the smell of burned wood. He saw a narrow, muddy lane flanked by dense trees. Rays of the setting sun scattered through the branches, painting the landscape in hues of orange and gold. However, the beauty did not last long as the sight of burned fields—likely set ablaze by Southern farmers before the war to prevent Northern soldiers from stealing their crop.

Suddenly, a dog began chasing the truck, barking loudly. Curious, Elias leaned out of the back to catch a glimpse, as the window was too small.

The dog was brown, its fur long and so thick. It looked strikingly familiar. Elias narrowed his eyes and began to wonder.

"Wait... is that Jai? The South Asian dog I met in the South? What is he doing here?" he whispered, and his eyes filled with tears and flashback of the south was evident on his face.

Elias banged on the truck walls, shouting, "Stop the truck now! Hello, can you hear me?"

The old, grumpy driver didn't hear Elias' voice but noticed the banging. He stopped the truck and opened the back.

"What is it now?" the driver grumbled and scratched his chin, his tone as rude as his expression.

Elias fumbled, embarrassed, but managed to speak with a nervous smile. "Th-the dog! I know him. I wa—I want—"

Before Elias could finish, Jai jumped onto the truck, tail wagging with happiness and excitement.

The driver sighed and rolled his eyes. "Whatever. Ugh," he muttered, returning to the driver's seat.

He started the truck again, mindful of their surroundings. The area was hostile, and any moment could bring danger—whether from rebel groups or angry farmers. Burning the truck wouldn't be difficult, especially since it was just Elias and the driver inside.

After a quite long journey , Elias finally reached North Parserland.

XIII

Louder Comrades

The driver opened the back lid of the truck.

"Here we are, comrade. Now begone at once—I've urgent matters to settle!" he said with his usual unwelcoming expression.

"Yeah, well, thank you, comrade," Elias replied.

He grabbed his coat, carefully placed the Secwrite inside his bag, and secured his gun to his shoulder using a piece of cloth.

"All right, comrade Jai, come on. Here starts your new journey," Elias said with a faint smile. Though exhausted and weary, he felt a sense of security with Jai by his side. For the first time in a long while, he felt he had a purpose—someone to accompany him on his journey. It was obvious Elias was glad to have Jai here.

Jai followed Elias out of the truck.

Elias inhaled deeply, letting the air fill his lungs. A few meters ahead, he noticed someone preaching. Beside the preacher stood a newer version of the speaking machine, loudly amplifying his words.

The preacher declared:

"North is the essence of communist blood that thrives within all citizens. The party is everything to us—no other relationship is greater than the party. It's just the supreme leader and us, the workers, serving them!"

"They've started hiring preachers now? Are they afraid people will eventually uncover the ultimate truth about the NSPP or what?" Elias chuckled, scratching his head.

He tried not to dwell on the events of his time in the South, instead distracting himself with the scenes unfolding around him. He glanced at random passersby, trying to engage with his surroundings.

An old lady walked past Elias, whistling a tune. It was a very old song Elias remembered hearing in his childhood. He smiled at her, but the old lady was so absorbed in her whistling that she didn't notice him.

Elias sat down in front of Jai and began talking to him. "That was quite an old song. It's nice to hear it; you don't often hear tunes like that these days. All we get are these party-pleasing songs now. Ah, well. Let's get going—we need to hunt for some food. Follow me!"

After walking for a while, they finally reached a cafe. Elias's stomach growled with hunger, and so did Jai's. Without a second thought, they stepped inside as soon as they spotted it.

"At least we're better off here than in the South. But we don't have the same freedom they do," Elias muttered to himself. "I still can't forget Sofia's brave speech. The South had its own aroma of freedom and martyrs who died protecting their ideology."

The cafe's interior was decorated with all sorts of propaganda posters. It was clear they were desperate for more manpower to continue their assault on the South.

To prevent any signs of internal dissent, guards kept a constant watch over every place.

Elias sat in a corner, where there was only a single seat and a round table. A small radio beside the table played softly in the background.

"Comrade! What shall be your order? By the grace of our supreme leader, we have things to eat. Praise him, will you?" said the waiter as he approached Elias.

"Ah, yes, yes, comrade! Glory to our supreme leader. Now, will you take my order?" Elias replied, rolling his eyes in annoyance.

"Certainly, comrade," the waiter said, his tone overly cheerful.

Elias ordered beer, bread, and a warm bowl of soup. However, the waiter returned almost immediately with an apologetic expression.

"My apologies, comrade. The beer is no longer in stock. It might arrive in a few days, I suppose—by the grace of our sup—"

Elias cut him off mid-sentence, waving a hand dismissively.

"Yes, yes, our supreme leader! Thank you so much comrade. Can I at least get the bread and soup?" he sighed, his annoyance clearly visible.

"certainly comrade , right away" replied the waiter with a firm voice

Elias fed Jai some biscuits he had bought on his way to the cafe.

"You seem to enjoy it, huh? This is the only kind of biscuit we have here ,no fancy flavors. So, get used to it," Elias said, laughing faintly.

The waiter returned with Elias's order in no time. After all, how long could it take to fetch a simple meal of bread and soup? Elias, excited to finally have a proper meal after days of hunger, eagerly attacked the food.

But just as he began, the waiter interrupted.

"Wait, comrade! You're not going to eat like that, are you?" the waiter shouted.

"And how else am I supposed to eat?" Elias replied, his tone laced with annoyance.

"First, you must pray to our supreme leader, thanks to him that you're having such fine bread and warm soup in the midst of this war," the waiter informed.

"Is this some new rule or something? I've never heard of it," Elias asked, exhausted.

"It was announced by the speaking machine just yesterday," the waiter explained.

"Ah, yes, yes. Whatever." Elias let out a deep sigh before speaking mockingly. "Thank you, good supreme leader, for this magnificent meal. Truly, you are the greatest and the only one who can save us from this... scandal of war. Thank you so very much."

He rolled his eyes as he finished. his irritation was perhaps visible across his face.

"Now, can I eat it?" he asked, gesturing impatiently toward the bread.

"Mhm, you better be grateful! And don't even think about wasting a single piece," the waiter warned him.

Elias, ignoring the waiter, finally took a bite of the bread.

"What is this? It tastes like it's been stale for weeks!" Elias shouted, visibly annoyed.

"This is all we have! Better than the South having no food at all, right? All glory to—"

Elias cut him off mid-sentence.

"To our supreme leader," he said with a wide, annoyed smile.

"Let's try the soup at least. It smells decent and is still warm," Elias murmured to himself.

Taking a sip, he immediately spat it out.

"It tastes like petrol! Where did you even get this? Did you milk it from the speaking machine's belly?" Elias shouted again.

"Enough! Comrade! We will not tolerate another word against the rations provided to us by the grace of our supreme leader!" The waiter banged the table, his voice echoing with fury and his eyes blazing with rage.

This drew the attention of everyone in the café, including a soldier stationed near the entrance. Suspiciously they stared at Elias.

"Y-yes, yes… I apologize, comrade," Elias stammered, attempting to diffuse the situation.

Fifteen minutes later, Elias was still sitting in the café. He glanced at Jai, who was happily munching on the biscuits.

"Your biscuits must taste far better than this petrol soup," Elias said with a wry smile.

Looking around, Elias remarked, "I kind of like the ambiance here."

The soft crackling of the radio beside him played an old, familiar tune—albeit altered with party propaganda lyrics. Despite the edits, the melody was soothing, calming Elias's mind. The café had an old-world charm, with its wooden furniture, waiters dressed in outdated Parserland uniforms, and ribbons of the NSPP's flag draped everywhere. The aroma of freshly brewed coffee filled the air, blending with the warm glow of the cozy yellow lights.

No wonder this place was often used for propaganda, Elias thought. Pictures of the café were distributed in the South via zeppelins to demoralize their enemies, showcasing the supposed beauty and prosperity of the North.

Elias checked the time—it was 9:15 a.m. The secretary's office opened at 10, and it was only a 10-minute walk from the café. Reassured, Elias remained calm, confident he would arrive on time to meet the secretary.

"We should get going now, Jai. Come on, let me introduce you to my friend Thomas," Elias said warmly.

Jai had become a comforting companion for Elias. His presence helped distract Elias from painful memories of the past—memories of Sofia's death and the horrors of the civil war. Still, Elias occasionally found himself lost in thoughts of Sofia, replaying her powerful speech in his mind.

It was strange to catch feelings so quickly, and for a Southerner, no less, Elias reflected. Yet Sofia's words lingered, haunting him. Her speech had been so powerful, so inspiring, that he couldn't help but wonder if the kind of freedom she spoke of could truly exist. If it did, then the so-called freedom he had in the North paled in comparison to the ideology the Southerners had been fighting to preserve for decades.

Elias was walking across the street, lost in thought, when a speaking machine nearly hit him. He hadn't noticed it while crossing the road.

The machine honked loudly, snapping Elias back to reality and saving him from a potential accident. He sighed deeply. "What a day... Goddamn. I just hope my meeting with the secretary turns out fine," Elias muttered.

His gaze shifted upward as two warplanes roared through the sky, locked in an intense battle—one from the

South and the other from the North. The sound of gunfire echoed across the town, and it was surprising to see a Southern plane reach this far into Northern territory. They must have had an exceptionally skilled pilot on board.

Elias noticed the Southern plane's design and recognized it immediately.

"Whoa! Is that... an Acentwaksif 98 A.F? Goddamn, those beauties from the civil war era. Look at it! Do you see it, Jai?" Elias asked, glancing at Jai, who barked in agreement.

Elias smiled faintly as he continued, his tone a mix of admiration and nostalgia.

"You know, Jai, the Acentwaksif 98 A.F was ahead of its time. It could hit a top speed of 331 miles per hour with 950 horsepower. Back then, it was nearly impossible to shoot one down—it zipped past enemy planes in seconds. And the firepower? Two 20mm cannons and two 7.7mm machine guns. It's amazing how much they achieved with it back then. But..." he hesitated.

"It's hard to believe it could hold its own against the North's Demon series planes today. Still, credit to the Southern pilot for defending themselves so well."

Despite the Southern pilot's skill, the Acentwaksif 98 A.F was ultimately shot down by the Northern plane. The crowd below cheered loudly for the Northern pilot, their enthusiasm filling the air.

"Those Waksif times are long gone," Elias murmured, disappointment clear in his voice. He couldn't help but recall how much he'd adored that plane series as a child. He'd even owned a toy model of the Acentwaksif 98 A.F, often pretending to be a pilot.

XIV
OFFICE OFFICE

At 9:45 a.m., Elias finally reached the office after being distracted so many times along the way. However, his mood had improved thanks to the lively atmosphere of the city. There was still some time left before the secretary arrived, so Elias decided to catch up with his friend Thomas. He was excited to introduce him to Jai, his dog, who wagged his tail enthusiastically in a rhythmic to-and-fro motion.

"War hasn't touched eastern Parserland yet—it's pretty quiet here. I like it," Elias muttered under his breath.

As he scanned the area, he spotted Thomas, as usual, flirting with Misty.

"Hey, Thomas!" Elias called out.

"E-Elias? My man, you're here! Come on up—Misty's giving us free tea today!" Thomas shouted back, grinning.

Elias rushed toward him, with Jai bounding behind.

"Haha! You fell for it again. Who's going to give you free tea in the middle of a war?" Thomas teased, while Misty giggled beside him.

"Bah, whatever! Meet my dog, Jai. I found him during my mission to South Parserland," Elias said, starting with excitement but ending with a touch of sadness that flickered across his face.

"Oh? A democrat dog, is it? Look, Misty—Elias is quite the rebel now!" Thomas joked, laughing.

"He's a fine-looking dog, but Jai is an unusual name. What were you thinking when you named him?"

"Well, I didn't name him," Elias replied. "A local told me his name is Jai. Apparently, his owner brought him here from South Asia. Maybe it's a common name there?"

"Yes! My aunt's distant relative lives in South Asia. They do have some unique names over there," Misty chimed in.

"Comrade Thomas, how about a real beer party at my house tonight? No more delays—you have to come this time. No excuses!" Elias said, laughing heartily.

"Aha, Comrade Elias, I should be the one saying that! Just last night, I went to your house with two fine beers, but your place was locked. You weren't back by then? So, I ended up drinking both near the elevator in your apartment building," Thomas said with a grin.

Elias stared at him dramatically. "You drank both beers alone?" he said, feigning a sob.

"Of course! I can drink gallons, comrade!" Thomas replied with a chuckle.

Misty burst out laughing, clearly enjoying the lighthearted banter between the two. Both Elias and Thomas were undeniably jolly and dramatic, making their company delightful.

Suddenly, Elias noticed the secretary entering the building.

"I've got to go now, Comrade Thomas and Misty. I have a meeting with the secretary. Could you take care of Jai while I'm in there? The secretary isn't a fan of dogs in the office," Elias said, straightening his coat.

"Yeah, of course! I'll look after this little Mr. Democrat. And about that meeting—well, I hope the secretary doesn't milk you dry in there," Thomas quipped with a mischievous smirk, glancing at Misty.

Elias followed the secretary to his office, knocking in the spy pattern before entering.

He stepped inside, greeted by the usual dark office and the old grumpy man sitting at his desk. But wait—was he smiling this time?

That's unusual, Elias thought.

"Come in, comrade, come in. I've been waiting for you," the secretary said, smiling warmly.

Woah, he's smiling? I can't believe this at all. Either I'll be fired today, or I'll be promoted, Elias thought nervously, wiping sweat from his forehead.

"You did an amazing job, Elias. Words can't describe how thankful we are—yes, even the supreme leader himself! Because of you, the new head of the Southern rebellion lies dead. When we bombed the house you marked through the mighty Secwrite, many of their prominent leaders were meeting to retaliate against us. But now? They all lie dead with just one strike," the secretary said, his tone brimming with triumph.

"Th-they all lie dead?" Elias repeated, the words sticking in his throat. His body froze as regret poured over him. Sofia's face haunted his thoughts, her voice echoing in his mind. The brave legacy of the Southerners... all gone? Their ideology, their future... who will lead them now? A storm of guilt and questions clouded his expression.

"Yes! They all lie dead, as per our information," the secretary continued, oblivious to Elias's inner turmoil. "We can never thank you enough, Elias. You are a hero for the North, and I shall reward you publicly. In the main square of East Parserland, with the giant NSPP screen for all citizens to see, we will showcase your bravery in this mission."

Elias froze, expressionless, gazing at the secretary as if a snake had just smelled him. A loud noise from a passing speaking machine snapped him back to reality.

"I—I am honored to have this privilege, Comrade," Elias said, straightening his posture and speaking in the most formal tone he could muster.

"Good. It will commence next week, so prepare a strong speech. All of East Parserland will be listening to you!" the secretary declared.

"Certainly, Comrade. Certainly!" Elias replied.

"Oh, and one more thing I forgot to mention, Elias," the secretary added with a hearty laugh. "You are being promoted from the spy department to the Nationalist Department. They handle traitors, and from now on, you'll be working there. It's one of the greatest privileges—this department ranks just below mine!"

"Th-thank you so much, Comrade. I cannot thank you enough. All glory to our supreme leader," Elias said, bowing before leaving the room.

As soon as he stepped out, Elias began making his way to the Nationalist Department, located three floors above in the same building. Strange screams could often be heard from there, but everyone conveniently ignored them.

Elias entered the lift, which creaked and groaned with its usual noises.

"Ah, finally! I feel so... happy? The day hasn't been great so far—especially with that horrible soup, ugh! I'll never forget that taste," Elias thought as the lift ascended. "But life here isn't all bad, is it? I stayed loyal to the Party, even knowing it's wrong, and now I'm promoted. I'll earn a fortune. How bad can it be to keep pretending?"

The lift doors opened, and Elias stepped out with curiosity and energy, eager to see his new workplace.

The area was brightly lit, with all sorts of propaganda posters plastered across the walls—many of which Elias had never seen before. Numerous flags waved gently in the room, though there seemed to be no breeze. Oh, wait—there was a fan below them.

The strange sounds of people screaming in pain grew louder. The sickening noise of someone being torn apart, perhaps by their legs, sent shivers down Elias's spine.

"Hey! You must be Elias?" one of the employees greeted him.

"I'm John, your new head. I'll give you a tour," John said with a smile.

"W-wait! What's that noise? Do you hear it too?" Elias asked, his voice trembling.

"That's none of your business, young man. You're not permitted in there—at least not yet. You'll gain access if you get promoted in this department, which isn't that hard," John replied firmly.

"Oh... I see," Elias muttered, his unease growing.

But those strange noises lingered in Elias's mind, captivating and unsettling him.

John showed Elias around the office. It was quite similar to the spy department, except for the abundance of propaganda plastered on every wall.

"All right, I'm leaving now. Do your work, and you can head out when you're done," said John.

"Oh, and one more thing—you'll be the last to leave the office because you're new. You'll need to clean all the senior desks before leaving, comrade," John added with a sly wink.

"Ah, certainly, comrade," Elias replied firmly, though his mind was buzzing with frustration.

The audacity of him to order me to clean desks and then call me a comrade! Doesn't comrade mean we're all supposed to be equal? Whatever. I'm more interested in my salary increment than this ridiculous task, Elias thought, gritting his teeth.

As Elias stayed behind, his mind wandered to Jai. What's Jai doing right now? Should I bring him up here? He must be feeling lonely, he muttered to himself.

Just as he was about to leave his chair, he noticed Jai standing at the door, startling him.

"You figured out how to use the lift, huh?" Elias asked, his voice laced with surprise and an awkward chuckle.

"Yes, I did!" came a response, leaving Elias frozen in disbelief.

"What? You can talk now?" Elias stammered, his heart racing.

"Stupid! It's me, Thomas!" Thomas burst out from behind Jai, laughing uncontrollably. Misty, standing beside him, doubled over in laughter as well.

"Ah, I couldn't help missing you, Comrade Elias, so I came up to scare you with your 'talking dog,'" Thomas said, still laughing.

"You're so funny," Misty said, rolling on the floor in fits of laughter.

Elias sighed, a grin at his lips.

"Don't forget us, all right? You're in this prestigious department now. Make the most of it," Thomas said with a genuine smile.

"Why would he? He's the one who ventured into the 'savage cannibal South,'" Misty teased.

Bah, that nonsense propaganda about the South. I just read it yesterday, Elias thought to himself, shaking his head.

"Yeah, yeah," Elias replied with an awkward laugh.

"Well, we'll get going now, Elias. Duty calls," said Thomas.

"And here's your 'democrat dog,'" Misty joked, handing Jai over.

"Shhh! Don't say that word so loudly! This isn't the spy department—it's the NATIONALIST department!" Elias hissed, glancing nervously around.

"sorry-sorry" grinned misty

After working for hours, surprisingly, Jai was just sleeping beside Elias and didn't make any noise at all, which made him happy. Maybe his office will accept him soon, he thought.

"Ah, time to go. Everyone's already left. It's so quiet in here... quiet offices are so peaceful," Elias wondered aloud.

Soon, the same screaming noise captivated his attention.

"You hear that, right? Let's go. No one's at the office—let's uncover what they're hiding. Perhaps I'll find a clue? After all, I was a spy," Elias smirked.

He approached the gate, each step silent, calculated.

The gate was massive and old.

"Wait! The key... let me try the master key John gave me to lock the office," Elias murmured, searching his pocket.

"Here it is," he said, excitedly, though his hand trembled slightly as he inserted the key.

The door creaked open.

The place was all dark and smelled as if something has been rotting since ages

Soon, Elias turned on his torch.

And what he saw nearly swept the ground from under his feet.

There were multiple prison cells—left and right—dimly lit, the flickering lights barely keeping the darkness at bay.

He took a few more steps, awe-struck, trying to take in more of the eerie place.

Then, a voice rang out from a few meters away—sharp, commanding.

"Hey! What are you doing here? Get out at once!"

Elias flinched, his heart pounding, and stumbled to the ground.

"M-My apologies, comrade! I... I didn't mean to come in here! It was just the v-voice..." he stammered.

The figure sighed.

"Comrade, it's me—Thomas! Stop apologizing and come outside," Thomas said in an exasperated tone.

"If it were anyone else, I would've reported them to the party. You'd have ended up in one of these cells too," he added coldly.

Elias exhaled deeply and finally stepped out, Jai trailing behind him.

"Well, well, no excuses! I know those voices are... tempting, but you must never disobey the party. I said never, ever. Or something far worse could happen..." Thomas warned.

"Mhm, my mistake for even checking it out. Thanks for covering for me—I hope no one else noticed," Elias muttered, still shaken.

Thomas just scoffed.

"I get it, I get it. Let's go have a drink at my place," Elias whispered.

"I'll need extra to calm myself after this," Thomas smirked.

It struck Elias as odd. Why was Thomas still in the office this late? He always left early...

As they stepped outside, they found themselves face-to-face with an NSPP rally.

Flags rippled in the air.

Men, women, children, elders—all chanting the party motto in unison. Banners tied across their heads, drums echoing through the streets.

They looked terrifying.

Yet somehow, under NSPP, they also looked... secure

Elias and Thomas discussed various thing about thomas' family , and his new born kid who is a total patriot , perhaps due to the nspp school , thy only feed propaganda in there

A speaking machine passed beside them, its mechanical voice blaring through the streets.

"South Parserland's most prominent city has been taken! I repeat—South Parserland's most prominent city has been taken!"

Elias startled, his breath catching. He turned to Thomas.

Thomas, however, looked back at him with unwavering patriotism.

At that moment, Elias knew—he and Thomas were worlds apart. Their thoughts, their beliefs, everything about them was different.

"Such a heartwarming piece of news. The beer will taste even better now," Thomas laughed.

"Inde-indeed, Comrade Thomas..." Elias muttered, hiding his disappointment.

"Comrade Thomas, can I ask you a question?" Elias asked.

"Mhm, why not?" Thomas nodded in affirmation.

"What do you know about those screams in the Nationalist Department?" Elias asked curiously.

"Nothing! What would I know about it?" Thomas shouted angrily.

Elias narrowed his eyes. "You mentioned something about prisoners, didn't you?"

Thomas rolled his eyes. "Yeah, so what? They keep prisoners there—people who defy NSPP's rules. The rest is none of your business."

"I see," Elias muttered under his breath.

"Look, a beer shop! I heard they have some good old ones," Thomas said.

"Let's get going then?" Elias replied.

The beer shop looked old and greasy, with a worn-out board outside—the faded text barely visible. Despite its shabby appearance, the shop sold quite well and was well-known among the locals.

A radio played in the background, filling the space with an old, soothing song:

"Oh dear hearts and harsh people..."

The melody had a certain charm, and Elias found himself captivated by it.

XV

HOME SWEET HOME

They finally reached Elias' home, carrying three bottles of beer.

Jai slept as soon as he entered the house.

"Come on now, put something good on the radio," Thomas said.

"Aha!" Elias replied, turning the dial.

Elias popped open a beer bottle, foam spilling slightly over the rim.

"Here we are," he said with a hearty laugh.

Thomas began talking about the fine woman he had married. She wasn't the best cook, but she was a devoted NSPP follower, which made her great in his eyes. She believed in extreme NSPP ideology—so extreme that even the NSPP itself had toned it down after the civil war. She also worked in the war department.

"She sounds like an amazing person. But if you're married, why do you flirt with Misty?" Elias asked curiously.

"Uh! Well... I... uh... never mind. Let's leave that for another day," Thomas fumbled.

"Let's drink to that?" Elias smirked.

"Cheers," both of them said in unison, clinking their bottles together.

After a few drinks, Elias leaned back and asked, "So, Comrade Thomas, tell me—how did you survive in the South during the great civil war? I clearly remember how we got separated in the midst of battle. I thought the Southerners had taken you prisoner or worse—tortured you to death. Dark times, those were."

"The dark times were never over, comrade. But by the grace of our supreme leader, I survived," Thomas said, his words slurring from the alcohol. "It was surprising—truly laughable—to witness the ignorance of the Southerners. They captured me, took me to prison... only to treat me like a war hero. Can you believe that? They interrogated me so gently, as if I were one of them. They were so foolish, they even believed my lies, comrade Elias."

Thomas let out a loud burp before continuing, "If a Southerner had been captured by the NSPP, their skin would have been peeled off, their legs torn apart in those smelly cells. We are smart. We always get the truth out of them. I wonder how long they'll even last once the second war wave begins!" He laughed heartily.

Elias was too stunned to react.

"W-wait, comrade," Elias stuttered. "What did you just say? About the cells? Are we really this cruel?" His eyes were fixed on Thomas, his breath unsteady.

Thomas hiccuped before responding, "Shit... I wasn't supposed to tell anyone. But well, I trust you, comrade. You won't tell anyone, right?" His voice wavered slightly.

"N-no," Elias fumbled, his hands clenching into fists.

"They deserve it," Thomas scoffed. "They are traitors to the supreme leader. We must always obey the leader. In fact, I think they deserve even worse... What about those fine Southern women? Maybe we should—"

Elias' mind instantly flashed to Sofia. His blood boiled.

"What? Are you out of your mind?!" he shouted, slamming his glass down on the table with a loud noise. "You're too drunk! Enough!"

Thomas grinned creepily. "Comrade, comrade... you're starting to sound like a rebel. I could send you to the cells too if I report this," he smirked.

Elias' face turned pale.

"But don't worry, comrade. It's just between us," Thomas continued, his smile widening. "You won't tell anyone what I said, right? Otherwise... people might start getting ideas, and we wouldn't want that, would we? Not as loyal party members."

Elias lowered his gaze, his heart heavy with disappointment and sorrow.

"I won't," he muttered.

Thomas, now too drunk to keep himself upright, slumped onto the floor and passed out. Elias tried shaking him awake, but he was completely unconscious.

With a sigh, Elias rushed to the caller machine, dialing Thomas' home number. When his wife picked up, he calmly informed her, "Thomas won't be coming home tonight. He drank too much and passed out."

While walking back home, Elias was lost in thought, his mind tangled with doubts about the party.

"It's not the Southerners who are ignorant... it's us," he realized.

How painful must it be—to be tortured like that? And for what crime? Defending their homeland? Even after everything, they still refuse to surrender, still fighting through the second wave. *Why?* What's so special about their ideology? Why don't they just give up?

A speaking machine rolled past him, its mechanical voice blaring through the streets:

"The Southerners are savage cannibals! They will eat you—your children—yes, you and your children!"

Elias stopped in his tracks. A cold wave of realization hit him.

Why are we even supporting the NSPP in the first place? It makes me feel safe... but for no reason at all. These speaking machines, the banners, the flags, the supreme leader's speeches—they all create an illusion of security. But in reality? I'm not safe at all. No one is. If I utter a single word against the party, I'm done for.

Then another thought struck him: *Why is this happening?* Why is no one standing up? *They can't kill all of us at once, right?* If we stand together, nothing is impossible. But convincing the people of the North? *That's another story.* They're too brainwashed, drowned in endless propaganda.

There has to be a way.

I can't leave the North—the South is unlivable for someone like me. It's war-torn, chaotic... depressing. But if what Sofia said in her speech was true, then there is nothing greater than what they're fighting for.

There has to be a way to convince the North, to expose what the NSPP is truly conspiring. But for that, I need more evidence—real, undeniable proof. Against the party. Against the leader.

Before he knew it, Elias had reached home. His hands trembled as he unlocked the door. His entire body was shaking.

He did not sleep that night.

Instead, he lay awake, his mind racing with plans, doubts, and fears. *How can I convince the people?* What if I lose everything? What if I end up rotting in a prison cell? Or worse—what if no one believes me?

One slip, one moment of suspicion, and it would all be over.

XVI

MY PEOPLE , MY COUNTRY

Elias woke up to the usual alarm.

"Ah, I hate this... I hate this," he sighed, rubbing his eyes.

His gaze shifted toward Thomas, who was still passed out on the floor. Elias crouched down and shook him lightly, trying to wake him.

To his surprise, Thomas finally opened his eyes.

"Well, comrade, I guess you had too much beer last night, huh?" Elias chuckled, not wanting Thomas to recall their conversation from the previous night.

"Yeah, I suppose... My head feels heavy," Thomas groaned, holding his forehead.

"Oh, Thomas... answer me, do you remember anything from last night?" Elias asked cautiously.

"No, I don't. How am I even supposed to remember that?" Thomas replied.

Elias felt a wave of relief.

But then, Thomas motioned for Elias to come closer.

As soon as Elias leaned in, Thomas suddenly grabbed his tie and pulled him close to his face.

He whispered in Elias' ear, "I do remember it. I remember it all."

Elias felt a shiver crawl down his spine.

"Don't you dare tell anyone. Understood?" Thomas continued, his grip still firm.

"Y-yes, I know," Elias fumbled his words.

"Good boy," Thomas smirked before pushing Elias away and walking out of the house.

He slammed the door behind him.

Thomas had changed completely. The party had consumed his mind, body, and very ability to think for himself.

However, it was better for Elias to stay silent—speaking up wouldn't end well for him.

Trembling, Elias sat there, shaken by the transformation of his childhood friend. He had never imagined Thomas would end up like this.

"I hope that one day, I'll be able to convince everyone to stand against the party. But the problem is, I don't even know where to begin. The party isn't just a name—it's a massive, complex hierarchy. Every single thing in Parserland is interconnected with the decisions of the party members," Elias thought, his mind clouded with uncertainty.

He sighed. "I should get ready for work. I'm already drawing too much suspicion these days. I can't afford to be late. I *can't.*"

Forcing himself to move, Elias walked toward his wardrobe.

He grabbed his coat, threw it on, adjusted his tie, and turned to the mirror.

He tried to smile. But he couldn't.

Instead, tears poured down his face.

His parents' deaths in the civil war, Sofia's execution, the endless butchering of innocents... and now, even his childhood friend had turned against him.

It was too much to bear.

His legs gave out, and he slumped into the corner of the room, sobbing uncontrollably. There was nowhere to lean his head, no one to confide in.He was completely alone.

Jai, who had just woken up, rushed toward Elias, expecting food. But seeing him cry, the dog simply sat beside him, leaning his head against Elias' leg in silent comfort.

Soon, Elias stood up and murmured, "I can't waste another second."

He gave Jai some food while preparing his documents for work.

As he glanced in the mirror, he noticed the dark circles under his eyes—evidence of countless sleepless nights. But it didn't bother him. Taking a deep breath, he finally mustered the courage to leave the room and head toward the office, knowing he'd have to face Thomas again.

On his way, he observed the people around him—their behaviors, their devotion.

A young man stood before a tattered poster on the wall, saluting it with unwavering loyalty, simply because the party's motto was written on it.

An elderly woman marched down the street, shouting praises of the supreme leader as if it were a prayer.

A mere eight-year-old was engaged in a fistfight, fueled by rage—his opponent had dared to speak against the party.

A teenager stood at a street corner, handing out the party's latest manifesto, filled with promises of Parserland's "glorious development."

Elias sighed. Everyone's life now revolves around the party.

"I see no love, no compassion, no kindness," he thought. "I am drowning in a sea with no end in sight."

Soon, Elias reached his office. It was an unusual yet expected sight—neither

Thomas nor Misty were waiting for him. It was unexpected yet, in a way, not surprising.

Stepping inside, he saw the usual banners being taken down and replaced with new ones. He walked a few steps further and spotted Thomas at his desk, already immersed in work. Their eyes met for a brief moment. To Elias' surprise, Thomas smirked at him—something that left him puzzled. Choosing not to react, Elias simply continued walking towards the lift to access the Nationalist Department.

"How does Thomas even know about the secrets of the cell if he's never been there? Strange..." Elias wondered.

The lift doors opened, and for a moment, a sense of dread crept over him. What if someone saw me entering the cell last night? But as he stepped in, no one confronted him about it. So, most likely, no one did

Elias reached his desk and powered on his computer. As always, Jai followed him, wagging his tail. Just then, a blonde woman, with sharp Northern Parserland features and seemingly around Elias' age, approached him.

"I wonder what she's up to... Did she see me enter the cell?" Elias thought warily.

"Hey, cute dog! You must be Elias, right?" the woman asked, her tone casual.

"Y-yes, that would be me. How may I help ya?" Elias responded, fumbling slightly yet keeping his voice firm.

"Nothing much. Just here to hand over your files and today's assignments. Long live the leader," she said, placing the documents on his desk.

"Aha! Was just waiting for them," Elias replied, forcing a small smile

The woman lagged for a moment or two, before glancing at Jai. " what's your dog's name?" she asked with a wide grin on her face.

"He's Jai," Elias replied simply.

Jai immediately started jumping around her as if they were old friends.

"Aren't you an adorable one?" she chuckled, scratching behind his ears.

"Well, Elias, I'll be off now. We'll meet later," she said with a playful wink.

"Yeah... sure," Elias replied, still somewhat distracted.

His mind was already weighed down by countless thoughts, so he didn't dwell on the conversation for long. He even forgot to ask her name. Instead, he focused on his work, determined to finish early and leave.

One benefit of working in the Nationalist Department was that those who completed their tasks ahead of schedule were allowed to leave early. But with the sheer amount of work assigned, very few ever managed to.

Just as he was settling in, a loud, piercing scream echoed through the office—the same scream he had heard the night before.

Elias tensed. His eyes darted around the room, scanning his coworkers' reactions. But to his shock, no one even flinched. It was as if they hadn't heard a thing.

Another ordinary day in the office.

Pushing the thought aside, Elias powered through his work and managed to finish by 4 PM. As he got up to leave, he could feel the jealous stares of his colleagues. However, he kept his gaze fixed on the door.

Taking the lift down, he reached the ground floor and stepped outside. He had barely walked a few steps when—

"Finished?"

A voice from behind made him freeze. Elias' heart pounded in his chest. Without turning around, he blurted out, "Yes, I did! I submitted the files—just let me go, ple—"

The voice felt familiar. Slowly, he turned around.

"Ah! Th-Thomas..." he stuttered.

"Yes! THOMAS," Thomas repeated with a laugh.

"Great, then. Go ahead... Or shall I come over to your place again tonight? We'll have some fine wine and talk some more," Thomas said with a smirk and a knowing wink.

"No, I'd rather not... not today," Elias muttered before walking off, his pulse still racing.

On his way home through a different lane, Elias's attention was caught by an old radio shop. It looked ancient, its doors appearing as though they belonged to another century. The songs playing inside could be heard from a few meters away, filling the air with a melody that sent a strange sense of calm through his nerves.

Without much thought, he stepped inside and approached the seller.

The shopkeeper was as old as Elias had expected. His long white beard reached his chest, while his hair was dyed black. He wore an outdated yet elegant suit, giving him a certain classiness, though his face carried a warm, approachable expression.

"Comrade, I liked the music that was playing just now. Do you have those cassettes available?" Elias asked.

The old man coughed lightly. "That's surprising," he said. "Young folks these days don't even come near this shop. All they listen to now are those soulless propaganda songs. I'd be honored to sell you the cassettes—and you know what? I'll even throw in a few more songs as a gift. And since you seem to appreciate good music, I'll give you a discount too." He smiled warmly.

Elias froze for a moment.

"Wait... did he just criticize the government? Did he? So, I've finally found someone who might be against the party too? Or am I reading too much into this? Maybe he's just talking about the songs. Should I ask him about his views on the NSPP? But if he's actually a party supporter, I could get into trouble..."

"Comrade? Where are you lost?" the old man asked, snapping Elias out of his thoughts.

"Ah—sounds great!" Elias replied quickly, forcing a smile.

"Here's the song list. Pick the ones you want." The shopkeeper handed him a paper with a checklist of available songs.

Elias, unfamiliar with old music, simply asked the man to give him the songs he personally liked.

The old man nodded and handed him a small stack of cassettes.

"Thank you, comrade. Please visit again, will you? And that'll be five parsers in total," the old man said, coughing again.

Without hesitation, Elias took out five parsers and handed them over.

Just as he turned to leave, a thought struck him.

"Can I ask you something?" Elias said.

"Of course, lad. What is it?" the old man replied.

Elias hesitated. "It's just... uhh..." He hesitated before finally asking, "What's your opinion on the NSPP?"

The old man realized his mistake—he had just criticized the party. His smile faltered for a fraction of a second before he quickly forced it back. A thought crept into his mind: *What if this young man works for the government? What if he was here to arrest me?*

Forcing a smile, he said, "I'm an old man—I don't even know if I'll see the morning tomorrow. So, in the end, my views don't really matter."

"Y-yeah," Elias muttered, then turned and walked out of the shop, Jai following close behind.

On his way home, Elias decided to buy something for dinner. He bought a loaf of bread and a handful of biscuits for Jai, from the bakery. The bread looked stale, and the biscuits seemed already expired, but there was nothing he could do. He had no other choice but to buy them rather than stay hungry tonight.

It was already 7 PM. While walking, Elias discovered a lonely path where no one else was. It was covered with grass and bushes. He hesitated to enter at first, but something about its beauty captivated him.

"Where does this lane lead? Looks like an entrance to the forest," wondered Elias.

He walked a few kilometers inside. It was getting darker and darker. His mind was tangled with thoughts of Maria, his first love, and how exactly he had lost her. Then, something unusual caught his eye—a caller machine.

"Wait? Is that a caller machine? What is it doing in the middle of nowhere?" Elias wondered.

He ran toward the machine and pulled the door open. The usual creak of an old door filled the silence. This caller machine looked far older than the others in town. However, it was still working.

Elias frantically searched his pockets, breathing heavily, panic setting in. Sweat dripped down his face as he struggled to catch his breath. His hands trembled as he pulled out Maria's letter—the same torn paper with three missing digits.

He had dialed this number so many times before. Yet tonight, he tried a new combination, one he had never attempted. He checked his diary, where he had recorded every failed call. A small hope still lingered in the corner of his mind, pushing him forward.

He cleared his throat, trying to suppress the fear that the call would fail again.

His eyes filled with tears as his hands shook. A panic attack hit him like a wave.

The dialer made a ringing sound.

A sharp pain struck Elias' chest, his heart racing at that very moment.

Then, the ringing stopped.

Elias held his breath, convinced that someone had picked up.

"Hello, Maria! I know it's you! It's me, Elias!"

The caller machine's robotic voice replied coldly:

"The number does not exist. Please try again with a different number or recheck it. Long live the Leader , The workers rise, the economy drives, the country thrives.."

The line disconnected.

Elias' heart shattered.

"Maria... it's me... E-Elia—Maria!" he cried out, his voice breaking. *"Remember me? Maria, it's me. I'm still waiting!"*

But deep down, he knew he was speaking to no one. His subconscious mind made him believe Maria was on the other end.

Tears streamed down his face. He clutched his hair tightly, his body shaking.

A scream tore from his throat, filled with anguish. The pain in his chest was unbearable, suffocating. He felt like he was dying.

Jai was waiting outside, barking anxiously as the door was locked from the inside.

The poor soul couldn't help Elias, no matter how much he wanted to.

Elias soon noticed Jai outside. Though he could barely move, he somehow managed to unlock the door. The moment he did, he collapsed onto Jai, hugging him tightly.

"I don't have anybody else in this world... it's only you," Elias sobbed, holding Jai even more firmly.

Exhausted, he lost consciousness, crying inside the caller machine. An hour passed.

During a routine patrol, a few policemen noticed someone asleep inside the booth. One of them poked Elias with a stick to wake him up.

Jai, who had curled up around Elias, stirred but didn't move away.

Elias' eyes fluttered open. He gasped, startled by the harsh glow of torches shining directly into his face. Fear gripped him.

"Who is it? I... I can't see you," Elias fumbled.

"Police. Department of Security. What are you doing here at this hour, huh?" one of the officers demanded.

Elias sat frozen, his mind racing. He didn't know what to say.

One of the policemen scoffed. *"Tch. He's probably drunk."*

"You! Get out of here. Stop boozing around like a fool. Leave now, or we'll arrest you," another officer barked, striking Elias with his stick.

Jai growled and tried to shield Elias, but it was useless.

Elias let out a pained cry as the stick hit him. Gritting his teeth, he forced himself to stand, summoning whatever strength remained in his body. Without a word, he turned and walked away.

"People are crazy these days. He's probably just another drunkard," one of the policemen muttered, laughing as he chatted with his fellow officers.

Elias barely able to walk , reached his home at midnight somehow , and fell on the floor and slept as soon as he opened his door.

XVII
What About This?

Elias woke up at his usual time for work, realizing he had slept on the floor with the door still open. He sighed, reaching over to turn off the alarm. His body felt stiff, but his mind was clearer than before.

He fed Jai, put on his coat and tie, and prepared to leave. Despite everything that had happened the previous day, he felt oddly optimistic.

"Come on, Jai," he muttered, motioning for the dog to follow.

As he was locking the door, a loud noise from outside caught his attention. His hands froze. Something was happening.

Rushing downstairs, Elias pushed through the entrance to get a better view.

His breath hitched.

In the middle of the street, soldiers were dragging someone through the dirt—his colleague, Comrade John. Blood and grime covered his face, his uniform torn, exposing bruised skin. A thick rope was tied around his neck, restricting his movements but not choking him completely.

John thrashed, his voice thick with terror. "E-Elias! Help me! They're arresting me for no reason!"

Elias' instincts kicked in. "STOP RIGHT THERE!" he shouted.

The soldiers turned, eyes narrowing at the interruption.

Elias quickly pulled out his Nationalist Department ID. "I demand to know the reason for his arrest!"

A soldier, nearly six feet tall and clad in full armor, stepped forward, smirking as he slowly approached. His polished rifle gleamed under the faint morning light.

"Is he your friend?" the soldier asked.

"No, but he's my colleague. And as an NSPP officer, I have every right to ask," Elias replied, his voice edged with frustration.

The soldier let out a low chuckle. "Calm down, comrade. This colleague of yours was caught criticizing our great Supreme Leader. How dare he, right? We're simply doing our duty. I assume you won't be standing in our way?" His smirk widened.

"No, I didn't!" John cried out. "Elias, listen to me! I was just gambling at the café—"

"Shut up! Not another word, or I'll cut off your tongue!" the soldier barked.

John trembled but kept trying to explain. "I was gambling... I lost, and I swore out of frustration. But the timing was just perf—"

A sickening thud echoed as the soldier struck John's head with the butt of his rifle.

John collapsed, unconscious.

The soldier turned back to Elias. "We'll be on our way now, comrade. Long live the Supreme Leader!"

Elias' throat felt dry. He barely managed to get the words out.

"Y-yeah... Long live the Leader."

The soldiers resumed dragging John through the dirt, their laughter echoing as they disappeared down the street.

Elias clenched his fists, but there was nothing he could do against fully armed soldiers.

Without a word, he started walking toward his office, forcing himself to act normal. Any sign of hesitation or concern could raise suspicion. Still, the helplessness gnawed at him—why couldn't he save John?

A speaking machine rolled past, blaring propaganda:

"They will kill your children. They are ruthless. They eat each other. Who could they be? Yes, you guessed it—the South!"

Elias barely reacted, sighing as he pressed forward.

After a few more minutes of walking, he finally reached his office.

Misty stopped him midway up the stairs, blocking his path. "Thomas is on leave today," she informed him. "So don't bother looking for him."

Elias immediately realized something—Misty knew nothing about his conversation with Thomas the previous night. That meant Thomas hadn't spoken to anyone yet. Relief washed over him, but unease lingered. Thomas now held power over him, the kind of power that could consume a person—just like termites slowly devour wood.

Choosing the stairs over the lift, Elias made his way to the Nationalist Department.

Before he could reach his desk, the department's head secretary intercepted him. "Comrade Elias, I need a favor from you today."

One of Elias' colleagues was on leave, and it was his duty to conduct routine inspections of the prisoners held in the department's cells.

Elias knew he couldn't let this opportunity slip by. If he could access the prisoners, it might help him gather more evidence against the party.

However, it wouldn't be simple. The cells were heavily guarded by specially trained soldiers. Interrogating prisoners without arousing suspicion would be nearly impossible. He needed a plan.

Keeping his expression neutral, Elias nodded. "Understood, comrade. I'll handle it."

His body tensed as he headed toward the prison block, Thomas' horrifying descriptions of the prisoners' treatment echoing in his mind.

Just as he reached the entrance, he felt a sharp jab from behind. He flinched, turning abruptly.

"Yes, comrade?" Elias asked, forcing composure.

The department secretary stood before him, eyeing him with thinly veiled contempt. Without a word, he tossed Elias the key, smirked, and walked off.

As he disappeared down the corridor, Elias caught his muttered words: "What a stupid fool..."

Elias ignored it. He inserted the key into the lock. The familiar creak of the door sent a chill down his spine, reminding him of the first time he had entered the cells—all alone.

The stench hit him instantly. Rotting corpses. Blood. He recoiled, pressing a hand over his nose to keep from gagging.

Mustering his courage, he stepped forward. A fully armored special forces unit stood ahead, their steel plates gleaming faintly in the dim corridor.

"You John?" one of the soldiers asked.

"N-no?" Elias replied hesitantly.

"Then you must be John's substitute for today, I guess?"

It hit him then—his colleague on leave was John. The same John who had been arrested that morning. He hadn't made it to work, and most likely never would again. The office hadn't been informed of his arrest yet.

"Y-yeah! That would be me," Elias forced out.

"Get going, then," the soldier muttered.

Elias stepped past them. The stench grew stronger with every step. The corridor darkened. His pulse quickened.

Then, his eyes landed on a particular cell. A prisoner sat inside. Something about him made Elias stop. Without hesitation, he strode toward the cell and unlocked the door.

The creak of the hinges startled the prisoner awake. His eyes went wide in terror, and he let out a hoarse scream. He scrambled backward, pressing himself into the corner, trembling violently.

Elias took a cautious step forward. In the dim light, the prisoner's condition became painfully clear—his body drenched in blood, his skin raw and peeling.

But it was the tattered uniform that caught Elias' attention.

Southern Air Force.

Kneeling, Elias lowered his voice. "Calm down. I mean no harm."

The prisoner shivered, his breaths shallow.

Elias met his gaze. "How did you end up here?"

The prisoner swallowed hard. "I... I'm the pilot of Acentwaksif 98 A.F... I mistakenly crossed the border during a training exercise. Got caught in a dogfight... lost the battle..."

Elias' mind raced. So it was him. The same pilot from that dogfight—the one he had watched go down.

He survived.

Glancing around, Elias made sure no one was watching. Then, he reached into his bag and pulled out an old recorder.

"Can you talk about your experience?" Elias whispered.

The pilot hesitated. "You're not one of them, are you?"

"No. Trust me."

The prisoner exhaled shakily. He had no other choice.

"They... they tried to tear my arms apart," he choked out. "They do medical experiments on us. Sometimes, they force us to eat dead rats—hoping we'll catch the plague. Other times, they make us drink the blood of the dead, mixed with a handful of rice..."

His breathing grew heavier. "They... they even tried to peel my skin off. They're not human."

Tears streaked his face.

Elias placed a hand on his shoulder. The prisoner let out a sharp scream.

Footsteps.

Elias froze.

A soldier appeared at the cell door. "What are you doing?"

Elias forced a sneer. "Just checking on these bastards."

The soldier studied him, then grunted. "I see."

As the soldier walked off, Elias whispered, "I'll get you justice."

The prisoner clutched his stomach. "Please... before it's too late."

Elias stepped out of the cell before anyone else got suspicious.Top of Form

Bottom of Form

The smell was still intact. Barely able to breathe, Elias decided to walk out of the prison. He wanted to interrogate more prisoners, but first, he needed some fresh air before stepping back inside the cell.

He walked towards the balcony of the office, finding himself alone. Behind him, the constant clatter of typing filled the air, workers tirelessly punching away at their machines.

Elias took a deep breath and looked at the city scenery. Everything lay in ruins and rubble—only a few buildings were being renovated, and a handful of workers cleared debris from the roads. The idea of declaring another war so soon after the civil war made no sense. Perhaps this was the plan all along—to keep civilians dependent on the NSPP forever. Endless wars, endless control.

His eyes soon caught sight of something below. A group of teenagers in party school uniforms had surrounded an old man.

The man lay on the road as they kicked him, his frail body barely moving. He was covered in dirt from head to toe.

Elias couldn't hear exactly what the teens were saying, but they were clearly supported by the soldiers standing nearby. However, one phrase stood out through the noise:

"You old bastard, you're useless to us! You don't work—work, damn it! Say it! 'The workers rise, the economy drives, the country thrives.'"

The old man was too weak to respond. He tried to speak, forming words one by one, but his injuries left him barely able to move.

Elias clenched his fists and slammed them against the balcony railing, helpless "was the world always like this?" he questioned to himself.

The sky was crowded with aircraft, their engines roaring as they advanced southward. Below, the land trembled under the rhythmic pounding of soldiers' boots.

As they marched, they sang a newly published military song. The words echoed through the streets:

Help me, faith, fill me with love,
That I may die for my country,
That I may die for you,
That I may die to banish your fear of tomorrow,
To rid you of worry and madness.

Elias found himself humming along. The song was catchy, but the more he sang, the more he realized just how powerful the government was. Compared to them, he was nothing—less than dust. And yet, even dust could gather into a storm.

A colleague stepped onto the balcony beside him. Elias didn't know his name, but the man seemed to recognize him. Everyone in the department knew who Elias was by now.

"Tired already?" the man asked.

If Elias had to describe him, he would say the man had a tired face, with dark circles beneath his eyes. He was older than Elias, his expression carrying a quiet exhaustion. His smile, though seemingly comforting, held countless untold stories beneath it—a mystery in itself.

Top of Form

"No, not yet. Just needed some fresh air," Elias replied.

"I see. Same here," the man said before straightening his posture. "But we shouldn't waste time standing around. Idle hands are for Southerners, not us! We have work to do." His voice was firm, almost rehearsed.

"Y-yeah," Elias sighed, then turned away, heading back toward the prison cells.

As Elias stepped inside, a guard stopped him.

"Inspection time is over. You can check on them tomorrow. For now, just patrol the area," gruffly he said.

Then, with a smirk, he kept one of his hand on Elias' shoulder and blurted out, "Long live the Supreme Leader, comrade!"

Elias hesitated for a second but quickly echoed the words back.

He walked deeper into the prison. The stench grew stronger with every step. The prisoners were in a miserable state—some barely looked human anymore. In one cell, severed hands lay discarded in a corner. In another, soldiers held a man down, peeling his skin away as he writhed. Some prisoners were covered in so many cuts and bruises that their skin was barely visible. Many didn't even scream anymore. They had no strength left to.

Elias couldn't believe what was happening right under their noses.

Carefully, he unzipped his bag just enough to slide out the camera. He adjusted it slightly, making sure only the lens peeked through the small opening. The dim lighting helped hide it. He zipped the bag just enough to keep it concealed, but still recording.

Elais walking went too deep inside the prison cells , it was quite terrifying , the floor was getting covered with blood

Suddenly, someone shouted from Elias' left.

"HEY, YOU!"

The voice was familiar, yet rough and aged.

Elias hesitated before turning his head. His heart pounded—he was recording everything, and even though the camera was well-hidden, the fear of being caught clung to him.

To his shock, it was Mr. Fistros.

Elias' eyes widened. A flood of memories from the South crashed into him—the rally, Sofia's speech, her death, the betrayal at Mr. Fistros' house. That same house where he had used the Secwrite to smuggle information right under their noses.

"Y-y-yes?" Elias stammered.

"Traitor!" Mr. Fistros roared. "You used us! You used Sofia! Because of you, the South is crumbling! All our leaders are dead—because of you, Elias!"

Tears filled in the old man's eyes. Seeing him break like that sent a sharp pain through Elias' chest.

"It's not like that! I—I'm trying to help—"

He stopped mid-sentence. If he spoke about his plan, a soldier might overhear. The cell walls made every word echo.

But Mr. Fistros didn't stop.

"You even took my only son's rifle! Do you have any idea how much he sacrificed for the South? How many righteous acts he carried out with it during the civil war? And you—" he spat on the ground near Elias, "—you are not even a fraction of the man he was. You will never be worthy of that rifle!"

Elias was overwhelmed.

A soldier came running and, without hesitation, slammed the butt of his rifle into Mr. Fistros' head. The old man collapsed, unconscious.

Elias stood frozen, too stunned to react. Moments later, Jai came dashing into the cell. Elias quickly ordered him to stay outside, sensing the place was unsafe.

But Jai's eyes caught sight of Mr. Fistros. Without hesitation, he ran toward the old man, wagging his tail. Mr. Fistros' head rested against the cold metal rails of the cell, and Jai, in an attempt to wake him, began licking his face.

The soldier, watching the scene unfold, grabbed the dog and yanked him away. Instinct kicked in—Elias rushed forward, his voice firm yet pleading. "This is my dog. I'm sorry. I'll take him away."

The soldier narrowed his eyes and grunted, "You better be."

Elias pulled Jai into a tight embrace. His voice dropped to a whisper, heavy with emotion. "Why did you come here? Why don't you understand? I have no one else in my life except you."

The same soldier, disgusted by the display, grabbed Elias and forcefully tore him away from his dog.

"It's work time, you scum! How dare you waste it on this nonsense?" he spat, his grip tightening. "Our supreme leader works day and night, and you? Worthless bastard!"

Without another word, he seized Jai and dragged him out of the cell.

Elias barely had time to react. Everything was happening too fast, slipping through his grasp before he could even process it.

Elias stood still , standing on his knees , looking down at the blood on the floor

It felt like he has been transferred to some other world.

He closed his eyes

A memory close yet distant hit him

There was once a park—he couldn't remember where, but he used to go there with his parents. Back then, there was nothing to fear, nothing to worry about. His friends would wait for him, eager to start their games. The sky, a soft blue, was speckled with small clouds, bathed in warm sunlight.

Then, one day, the civil war was declared. The sirens tore through the air, shattering the peace in an instant. He still remembered that day as if it were yesterday.

People ran in all directions, panic swallowing the streets. But Elias stood still in the park, trying to make sense of the chaos. In mere moments, the sky—once gentle and familiar—was devoured by warplanes, their engines roaring like a storm.

"Hey! What the hell are you doing, still standing there? Why don't you listen?"

The harsh voice yanked him back to reality. It was the same soldier, returning after locking Jai outside the cell.

Elias flinched, startled. He quickly got to his feet, forcing himself to move—to act normal. He couldn't afford to draw any more suspicion.

A loud bell rang through the prison block and Elias flinched. The sound was alien to him, a hollow, metallic resonance, which resounded only in these cells. It was the end of the working day, and it meant that those who worked in the deepest parts of the prison were now allowed to leave. Without hesitation, Elias took off, one hand over his nose, running towards the balcony. When he came out of the cell, Jai naturally followed him, thinking that Elias just wanted to leave the office. But that wasn't the case. Elias wasn't trying to leave for work; he was trying to leave the prison cell before his stomach exploded. He didn't even make it to the balcony before he leaned forward and vomited.

Day one, huh?" A chuckle sounded from behind.

Elias turned sharply. "Ah... Thomas. Wait, weren't you on leave?" he exhaled.

"Yes, your most beloved comrade Thomas. Aren't you happy to see me? I came just for you!" Thomas said with a smile that appeared warm yet felt oddly unsettling.

"I was just passing by and saw you struggling, so I thought I'd offer you a hand," he added casually.

"Whatever. Thanks for your help," Elias muttered, rolling his eyes with a mocking expression.

Thomas laughed. "Ahh, ah ah! I haven't forgotten what you said that night."

Leaning in with a smirk, he whispered, "Better not push me—I might just let something slip about you."

Then he turned and walked away, whistling a tune as he stepped off the balcony.

Elias stood still. It wasn't surprising—this was exactly what he had expected Thomas to say.

He sighed and started walking outside the office.

As he walked downstairs to leave, Misty came running toward Elias—a sight he hadn't expected. Her hair brushed through the air, her pale white skin glowing. Her feminine beauty was clearly visible.

She grabbed Elias' hand. "Come, I have to show you something."

She rushed outside the office, leading him to a massive crowd cheering for something. What could it be?

A stage stood outside the office, likely built during working hours, so Elias had no idea what was happening. The crowd roared the supreme leader's name, party slogans echoed all around, and people threw flowers from their terraces. Was this some kind of god's arrival?

Is the supreme leader visiting the office? Elias wondered.

He anxiously scanned the area for clues, then sighed. Why not just ask Misty? She was standing right beside him. That's when he noticed—she was still holding his hand. It made him a bit nervous, but he chose to ignore it.

"Hey? What is all this? Why the crowd?" Elias shouted over the noise.

Misty looked at him in disbelief. "You don't know? Seriously? That's ridiculous! Didn't you hear the speaker blaring since afternoon?"

"I was in the cell. How was I supposed to know?" Elias replied.

"Oh, I see. Well—" Misty began, but her sentence was cut off as the crowd erupted in cheers, encouraged by the announcer.

"Of what?" Elias insisted.

"The South."

"The South?" Elias muttered. Wasn't Sofia the most prominent leader there? Didn't she die in front of me?

The whole scene replayed in his mind—the burning buildings, Sofia's face barely visible through the flames, the way she turned toward him one last time, the bullet that struck her, the blood, and the mocking laughter of the soldiers.

Elias' face went pale.

"What happened?" Misty shook his arm slightly, snapping him back to reality.

"N-Nothing... all glory to the supreme leader," Elias stammered at first but quickly firmed his tone.

"Sure we should!" Misty said, sounding impressed.

Elias observed how people fell in love these days. It wasn't an individual's beauty or personality that drew others in—it was how much they praised and remained loyal to the party.

Snapping back to reality, he focused on the stage, his anxiety growing. Who could it be? Who is the most prominent leader of...? His thoughts trailed off. Could it be Sofia? He questioned himself again.

No, it can't be. Sh-she was dead. He sighed, trying to reassure himself.

"The wait is over, comrades!" the anchor shouted with all the force he had.

"3... 2..."

The crowd roared in unison. "1!"

A large chest-like box creaked open. From within emerged a woman—her face concealed beneath a black cloth. Her figure was unmistakable, a curvy waist and a youthful frame.

Elias' heart pounded violently. The resemblance was too strong. No... it couldn't be. His breath hitched, his vision blurred. He felt like he might collapse at any moment.

"Shall I uncover her face?" the anchor bellowed.

The crowd erupted in thunderous affirmation.

Something inside Elias shattered. He clenched his fists, struggling to hold back his tears. He couldn't afford to break down—one crack in his mask, and everyone around him would suspect him.

But deep inside, all he wanted was to run to her, to beg for forgiveness. If only he could turn back time. If only he could do something—anything—to change this moment.

Suddenly, a dozen Acentwaksif 98 A.F warplanes from South Parserland covered the sky, their roaring engines so deafening that they drowned out the entire crowd's voices.

"Wait—what? How did the South get so deep inside North Parserland?" Elias was shocked, yet a flicker of excitement stirred within him. He desperately wanted the South to win, no matter what. But this? This was unexpected—defeating the North's formidable warplanes and penetrating so far past the border?

Panic spread like wildfire. First, countless pamphlets rained from above, covering the sky in a flurry of paper. Then, small objects—resembling bullets—dropped alongside them. Elias had no idea if they were dangerous, nor did the others. Fear seized the crowd, and people scattered in all directions.

The bullets hit the ground.

A thick smoke erupted, engulfing the entire area in an impenetrable haze. Chaos took over. A stampede broke out as everyone scrambled to save themselves. Misty clung tightly to Elias, but his focus wavered. He caught sight of the prisoner in the chaos—her features eerily similar to Sofia's. A wave of memories crashed over him, drowning him in the past. Without thinking, he loosened his grip on Misty's hand.

"D-Don't leave me—"

Misty's voice barely reached his ears before they were swallowed by the surging crowd. Elias found himself pushed toward the stage, barely managing to stay on his feet as the stampede raged around him. Regret clawed at him—he shouldn't have let go. But there was no time to dwell on it. He forced his way forward, determined. He had to save the prisoner.

People collapsed before him. Some were trampled underfoot. He stepped over lifeless bodies, his vision blurred by the thick white smoke. Nothing was clear—only an endless, suffocating fog.

Somehow, he reached the stage. His footing faltered, and he fell hard, pain jolting up his arm. His hand throbbed, blood trickling from a fresh wound. Gritting his teeth, he pushed himself up, grabbed the stage railing, and climbed.

Through the dense smoke, a black mask stood out. It was the prisoner.

"Come with me!" Elias yelled, grasping her hand.

He pulled her along, weaving through the madness, heading toward a place he knew—a silent, forgotten area where few ever wandered. The same place where he had once broken down in front of the caller machine, where he had encountered the police. At night, they patrolled it. But now, in the evening, it was deserted.

He took a moment of breath, steadying himself, and looked at her.

She pulled out the black mask.

Sofia.

The one Elias had been searching for. His worst fear, yet the one thing he couldn't stop wanting. And still, he wasn't ready to face her.

"You? You again?" Sofia's voice cracked as she screamed. "Let me die! I don't want to see you!"

Her face—barely recognizable, marred with deep cuts—was streaked with tears, pooling in the wounds, making them sting even more.

Elias moved fast, clamping a hand over her mouth.

"Shh! Don't scream!" he whispered ,yet firm. "You have no absolutely idea what they do to people in there. I know—I know I should be sorry for what I've done, but I don't have time to explain right now. J-just stay silent and come... if you still care about the Southerners."

Anyone could see the hatred in her eyes, the way disgust twisted her face.

Yet, with no other choice, Sofia went with him.

"Trust me... at least this last time," Elias said.

"I don't trust you. Not after what you've done."

A distant sound of marching soldiers rang in Elias' ears. He didn't have time to argue. He grabbed Sofia's hand again and pulled her with him, running toward his house.

No citizen would recognize her—her face had never been revealed to the public, which worked in their favor. But the soldiers knew her, and within days, they'd plaster her picture all over town.

They reached Elias' home at last. He rushed upstairs and shoved open the door. The journey back had been brutal—rubble from bombed buildings still choked the northern streets, making every step treacherous.

And then it hit him.

Jai.

Where was he?

Panic seized his chest. *Wait... Jai?! Where is he? Where is he?? Oh god, is he still in the office? Is he okay? Did—did he even survive the stampede?* His breath caught. *I hope he didn't go outside for God's sake.*

Elias screamed in helpless frustration.

"Wait... you even brought Jai from the South?" Sofia scoffed. "What, are you a thief too?"

"Can you just stay quiet for a while? Please." Elias's voice was strained, pleading.

Then—

A bark.

He froze.

"Is that... Jai?" His voice wavered with hope.

Without another word, he bolted downstairs. "Stay here. Don't move. Just—just stay here, I'll explain everything."

He flung open the door. And there, following the familiar path Elias always took, was Jai.

The dog had found his way home.

Elias dropped to his knees, his hands running in Jai's fur. "I'm sorry," he whispered, pressing his forehead against him. "I'll never leave you like that again."

Sofia watched from the window, disbelief written all over her face. *How could he care this much... for jai?*

She couldn't understand it.

XVIII
CONSPIRATION

Elias brought Jai upstairs, locked the door, and took a deep breath before turning to Sofia.

"Don't look outside! The soldiers might recognize you. Cover the window with the curtain, will you?" he said.

"Yes! And stop giving me orders, you scum," Sofia snapped.

"First, let me take care of your wounds."

"No. First, tell me why you're doing all this," she demanded, her voice laced with annoyance.

Elias opened his first aid kit, pulling out antiseptic cream and a few bandages.

"I'll explain while I treat these wounds. Alright?" he said.

"Whatever. Just don't try to outsmart me," Sofia muttered, rolling her eyes.

"Take it easy," Elias said as he dabbed the cream onto her wound.

"The thing is, I *do* have a bit of a brain. And yeah... I've realized I'm on the wrong side."

"Oh? So now you've *grown* a brain? After destroying the South's base, after leaving it on the verge of collapse—all because of *you*?" Sofia spat, disgust twisting her expression.

Elias let out a slow breath, trying to remain calm. "We can't bring back the dead, can we? Let's focus on how we can turn the tide of this war."

He picked up a bandage and wrapped it around her wound. She winced, biting back a scream.

"It'll heal soon," he assured her.

Sofia let out a bitter laugh. "*We can't bring back the dead, right?* Then let me die. I don't want to live in this world anymore. Why are you even helping me? I *know* this must be some dirty trick again. You should've left me with those soldiers—they would've given me an easier death."

"Oh? Is that what you think?" Elias asked, his voice firm. "That they would've just *executed* you and spared you the suffering? Then *see this*."

Jai jumped onto Sofia's lap, curling up against her. He had no idea what was happening—he was just happy to see her after all this time. Back in the South, Jai hadn't been particularly attached to her, but he *knew* her. She had fed him a few times.

Elias pulled out his recorder from his bag and removed the memory card. Without a word, he walked to the other side of the room and inserted it into the old television. He rarely used it—mostly because it only played propaganda channels, military anthems, and state-approved films.

"Is the remote beside you?" he asked.

"No? Where is it?" Sofia replied, not even bothering to glance around.

Elias sighed. "I can see it. It's to your left."

"Bah! Here." She grabbed the remote and tossed it carelessly toward him.

Elias caught it just in time, shaking his head. "Crazy," he sighed.

Then, without hesitation, he pressed 'Play.'

The video played. Its quality was poor, hazy with age, but still visible enough.

The sound of blood dripping echoed clearly—it was coming from the ceiling. The prisoners' conditions were horrifying; their skin was barely visible beneath layers of wounds and grime. Then came the most chilling part—the conversation Elias had recorded with Mr. Fistros, the moment he was silenced simply for making a noise.

"W-Wait... is that Mr. Fistros?" Sofia asked, her voice barely above a whisper.

"I'm afraid so," Elias replied.

Sofia's face turned pale. She couldn't find the words—only one thought escaped her lips.
"Th-That's horrible..."

A shiver ran down her spine. "How can someone be this cruel?" she added, almost to herself.

"I know, right? And this is my only lead to expose the Party. But I don't trust the people of the North. They might not believe me. Or worse... they might say those prisoners deserved it—that this treatment is justified."

Sofia swallowed hard. "That... that could happen, but how? How did you change so much? I can't believe you're the same person. I don't even know if I should trust you."

Elias let out a quiet sigh. "You see, when I first heard your speech in the South, I thought it was just another piece of Southern propaganda. But seeing how deeply you believed in it, how much it mattered to you—it had an impact on me."

Sofia was taken aback. A mix of shock and a strange sense of pride settled in her chest. She had somehow managed to change a man once devoted to blind obedience into someone who now questioned everything.

"Still," she said, regaining her composure, "don't think that means I trust you. Not after what you did there."

Elias smirked at her response. He could tell she was only pretending. He had nowhere else to go, and she had no intention of handing herself over to the soldiers below. Besides, that video had shaken her—whether she admitted it or not.

"Enough of this. We don't have much time, and keeping you here is dangerous," Elias said, his tone serious. "But no one will suspect me—not after my so-called great deeds. Well... not so great, actually."

Sofia narrowed her eyes. "What plan are you up to, huh?"

She was confused. She couldn't quite grasp what he was thinking or how he would even take the first step. Still, despite herself, she was keen to know—curious about what he had in mind.

"Plan, plan, plan... hmm..." Elias muttered. "Honestly? Even I'm not entirely sure what I'm up to. You see, the government keeps everything hidden from us—this torture of prisoners is just one example. For the love of God, I have no idea what else they've been concealing." He sighed, looking at Sofia.

He stretched out one arm, resting it on the table.

"You want to hear some music? I've got a few great tracks," Elias offered.

"Perhaps I'd be more delighted—no, honored—to finally hear your plan," Sofia replied, raising an eyebrow. "Because at this point, I have completely lost hope in this war."

"I see," Elias nodded before playing an old song, one he used to listen to at home.

"Ah, my plan! Well, you know, after my so-called great deeds in the South—well, sorry, not-so-great deeds—ah, apologies for the repetition," he chuckled.

Sofia sighed, exasperated. "Elias, this is not the time to joke around. Are you drunk?"

"Uh, no! Well... never mind, I did have a shot in the office courtyard," Elias admitted with a guilty smile.

"Oh, so that explains it," Sofia muttered. "Now, about the plan?"

Elias began pacing back and forth.

"Aha! I remember now. The Secretary is going to make a public announcement about my great deeds in the South—oh, never mind, not so—"

"Yes, yes! Not-so-very-great deeds in the South! I get it, Elias. You're driving me mad!" Sofia interrupted, rolling her eyes.

"Right, certainly!" Elias continued. "So, during the announcement, they're setting up a massive screen—specially ordered from the capital, mind you—and it'll broadcast my mission in detail, showcasing how I supposedly helped in the South."

Sofia cut him off again. "You know what? My blood is already boiling! Can you stop this nonsense—your babbling, your admiration of their so-called advanced technology—and just get to the point?" she hissed, keeping her voice low. She knew the consequences of being overheard.

"Let me speak, will you? Your kind, gracious madam," Elias said with a mocking bow.

Sofia huffed, crossing her arms.

"So, my plan is simple," Elias continued. "I'll load the videos I recorded onto that giant screen. The whole town will be gathered there—it's the perfect moment. If I play it right, I might just spark a rebellion... or perhaps even a civil war."

The way he spoke, anyone could see how much he craved the fall of the NSPP.

"But... they'll kill you in an instant! The soldiers won't let you get away with this," Sofia said cautiously.

Elias let out a short laugh. "Hah! What would I even do with this worthless life? I've seen enough days, Sofia. If I manage to change even one person's mind, that person will change another, and so on. Before you know it—boom! A civil war." He laughed heartily, but there was a flicker of fear in his eyes.

Sofia hesitated. "And what if you fail?" Her voice wavered slightly, her eyes softening. She saw how much Elias had changed. The man before her wasn't the same one who had helped destroy the South. A part of her thought—perhaps, one day, she could forgive him. But not yet. The horrors he had committed couldn't be erased so easily. Could they?

Elias sighed, lifting his hand off the table. "If I fail... I fail." His voice was flat, resigned.

"Well, before that, I have to think about your safety," he said, straightening. "The public doesn't know your face. That works in our favor."

"But won't the soldiers print posters? Stick them all over town?" Sofia asked.

She muttered under her breath, just low enough that Elias couldn't hear: "What a lunatic."

Elias smirked. "Do you think I'm stupid? Huh? I worked for the Party—the National Socialist Party of Parserland—for years." He leaned forward, his breath warm against her ear. "I know exactly how they operate."

Then he leaned back.

Sofia exhaled sharply. "Can you stop acting like you're the smartest person on the planet?"

"Well, you know what? Fine. Let me tell you then." Elias tapped his fingers on the table. "The Party isn't foolish enough to plaster your face everywhere. That would only lower public morale. Instead, they'll declare you dead—say you died in the stampede. They'll even produce a fake body as proof. The people will believe it. Meanwhile, the soldiers will keep hunting for you in secret. Not a single citizen will know what's happening behind the scenes."

He smirked, completely confident in his assessment.

"Oh? Is that so?" Sofia challenged. "In the South, something like this would never go unnoticed. People would take to the streets in protest." She said it with pride, making sure Elias understood how much more freedom the Southerners had.

Elias arched a brow. "Oh yeah? See for yourself."

He grabbed the remote and switched the television to the news channel.

The screen flickered. A solemn-faced reporter stood in front.

"The recent stampede—caused entirely by the bloodthirsty demons of the South—has left 45 dead. But do not worry! Our mighty, mighty Supreme Leader will have his revenge. The government is with you."

Sofia's fingers clenched into fists.

The reporter continued, a wicked smile curling his lips. "As for the prisoner? She died in a bombing—by their own planes! How foolish can they be? This just proves their shockingly low intelligence."

Then, to Sofia's horror, the reporter burst into laughter. And it didn't stop. The sound of his laughter echoed through the room—loud, forced, unnatural—stretching on for more than 15 seconds.

"Just as I mentioned," Elias sighed.

Sofia gave a slight nod, signaling her reluctant agreement.

"Perhaps you should rest? I'll go to the market and buy a few groceries for dinner. And do not—I repeat, do not—look out of the window. Also, check through the door's peephole before opening it. If it's not me, don't open it," Elias said firmly.

"Y-Yes..." Sofia stammered. She was too overwhelmed to process everything happening around her.

"See ya."

Elias grabbed his coat and stepped out. For a brief moment, he debated whether to lock the door. In the end, he decided to—better safe than sorry.

As he walked through the streets, unease gnawed at him. Had any soldier noticed him sneaking Sofia home? But no—he reassured himself. The soldiers had all been ordered to attend the execution ceremony. No one had been watching.

He exhaled deeply, trying to clear his mind. The sky was painted in hues of gold and orange as the sun dipped toward the horizon. A picturesque golden hour—yet Elias saw something else in the sunset.

The sun will rise tomorrow... with a new hope, a new beginning.

That single thought sent a surge of motivation through him.

The streets were eerily empty, dust swirling in the wind. Crumpled flyers, dropped from Southern planes, skittered along the ground. Soldiers scrambled to snatch them up, ensuring no civilian laid a hand on them. Anyone who tried was beaten mercilessly—an act of *disloyalty to the Leader*, as they called it.

A propaganda vehicle rolled past Elias, its speakers blaring the same scripted lines from the news broadcast. The same twisted narrative. Over and over.

Meanwhile, back at the house, Sofia fought an internal battle.

Could she trust Elias? Should she?

The question haunted her.

She had spent years loathing him, dreaming of vengeance ever since she learned his true identity. And now, after all that, he had the audacity to mock her with his so-called change of heart?

She paced the small room, lost in thought. Jai, as usual, was fast asleep.

"Jai hasn't changed a bit," she muttered with a faint smile. "He used to sleep all the time back there too."

Her smile faded as reality crashed back in.

No. I shouldn't trust him.

Her fists clenched.

I ought to take revenge. For the South. For all those who died because of this bloodthirsty bastard. I can't just let it go. I won't. I need to come up with a plan.

Elias reached the market, though the distance felt far greater than usual. His mind was under siege, thoughts swarming like vultures.

"Aha! Elias, come, come! Comrade, you have no idea how honored I am to see you here!" The seller, Comrade Steen, greeted him with enthusiasm.

"Mhm... true enough, Comrade Steen. Quite a rough day today. The news about the stampede was disheartening," Elias replied, forcing a look of disappointment.

In reality, he felt the opposite. Meeting Sofia had been a stroke of fortune—she would be an invaluable asset in executing his plan.

"Yeah... quite a loss." Steen sighed before shifting gears. "Anyway, how may I serve you today, comrade?"

"Nothing much, just the usual," Elias said, knowing Steen already had his regular purchases memorized.

As Elias waited, the Steen's wife approached with a steaming cup of tea.

"Ah, that wasn't really necessary, comrade. Thank you so much," Elias said, feeling both shy and grateful for the gesture.

"You don't visit often these days, Elias. Pay us a visit sometime. Our daughter is of marriageable age now... perhaps we could arrange a meeting. No rush, of course," the Steen's wife suggested warmly.

The seller hissed at her, subtly signaling her to drop the topic.

"I'll surely think about it. Thanks again for the tea, though," Elias replied tactfully. He didn't want to offend or dampen the conversation with an outright refusal.

"Don't thank me—thank the Supreme Leader," the woman said with a proud smile. "He granted the tea marketing bill, lowering prices by 1.5%."

"Ah! Yes, yes, I heard about that," Elias responded with a forced, faint smile.

"Here's your groceries, comrade." Steen handed over the items, placing them inside a polythene bag.

"I'll be going now, comrade. Here's the money." Elias respectfully handed over the cash.

"Uh... I fear this isn't enough, Elias. Prices have gone up a bit," Steen said hesitantly.

"Again?" Elias sighed. "How much more?"

"Just five parsers," Steen replied with a faint smile.

Elias searched his pockets, fishing out a few coins. He counted them, rolled his eyes, then tossed them to Steen before walking off.

A few minutes into his walk, his thoughts drifted to the soaring prices and the corrupt policies fueling them. *Steen's wife was so happy about the price of tea going down by a mere percent, yet they fail to see how everything else has shot up.* He let out a deep breath.

Upon reaching his building, Elias took the elevator up. He unlocked the door and gave a sharp knock before pushing it open, startling Sofia.

Realizing it was him, she exhaled in relief. "Wait—did you lock it from the outside?"

"Yeah. If anyone came by, they'd think no one was home and just walk away," Elias replied, exhaustion evident in his voice. It had been a long day.

"I'll go make dinner," he said, setting the bag down. "You go rest till then."

"I don't want to! I'll do it when I feel like it," Sofia exclaimed.

"Tell me more about your plan. Maybe I can help?" she added, her tone casual yet calculated. In truth, she wasn't looking to assist—she was searching for a weakness, a single flaw that could unravel Elias' entire scheme. Her priorities had shifted; she no longer believed anything could be done for the South, especially not by one man acting alone. Logic dictated his failure.

"Yeah, sure. At least I won't get bored while cooking," Elias replied with a soft, reassuring smile, completely unaware of the storm brewing behind those eyes watching him.

"Yeah, so... I don't have enough evidence at the moment," he admitted. "I'll be filming more prisoners, gathering testimonies of those who have suffered under the Party. But time is running out. The ceremony is at the end of the week." He sighed, exhaustion seeping into his voice—hopeful yet hopeless.

"Ah, I see," Sofia murmured, her interest sharpening.

"John was caught by the guards this morning—over something foolish, really. They replaced me in his position, and guess where that is?" Elias let out a dry chuckle. "In the prison cell itself. That should make things easier for me."

"Oh, that makes more sense now. However, one question arises in my mind, Elias," Sofia said, her voice carrying a persuasive charm that could convince anyone.

"Yeah, sure. What is it?" Elias asked.

"Does no one in all of Parserland suspect that you're secretly against the Party?" Sofia pressed, her curiosity genuine this time.

Elias hesitated for a brief moment. "Well... there is one," he admitted, fumbling slightly. "Thomas—my colleague. He's the one I fear most. But I'm not stupid. I know some of his secrets too, enough to keep him from exposing me. Still... that man is madness—pure madness. I fear that one day, in a fit of lunacy, he might 4reveal my true identity to the Party." He sighed, scratching his head with his left hand while stirring the pot with his right.

"Aha... here's my lead," Sofia thought, her mind racing. "If I can turn Thomas to my side, Elias' downfall is inevitable."

"E-Elias, I have one more question," she said, keeping her tone unchanged. "Does Thomas know about your plan?"

"Of course not!" Elias chuckled. "All he knows is a drunken statement I made while boozing at home. He doesn't have the slightest hint about what I'm actually conspiring behind the Party's back."

"That's it! The enemy's friend is my friend," Sofia muttered to herself.

"These days, it's easy to get someone caught. They don't even ask for evidence. I wonder how it is in the South?" Elias asked.

Snapping back to reality, Sofia nodded. *"Oh, yeah, yeah... In the South, evidence is necessary. You can't just throw anyone in jail."*

"That's exactly why I want the South to win this," Elias said, leaning back. *"All I can hope for is that my plan works—that a civil war erupts in the North itself. The government won't be able to do a thing if people unite. And even if I fail, it's still a victory for me... At least I won't have to live in this miserable world."* He sighed.

"Not so fast, Mr. Elias Vyane," Sofia smirked, thoughts swirling in her mind. *I have some scores to settle with you.*

"Mhm," she murmured absentmindedly.

"Well, here's your 'North Special Salad.' I'm too tired to cook anything else," Elias said, handing her a bowl of salad before heading toward the sofa.

"T-thanks... You're not eating?" Sofia asked.

"Nah, not hungry," Elias replied before lying down. He closed his eyes, making it clear that he wanted her to take the bed. He had no intention of making her uncomfortable by sleeping beside her.

Within minutes, he drifted into a deep sleep.

Sofia took a bite of the salad. *"Tastes way better than I expected,"* she admitted, mildly impressed.

Bowl in hand, she wandered around the house, thoughts racing. *Perhaps I can follow him when he leaves for his office tomorrow morning? But how? The soldiers will probably recognize me, won't they?* She sighed

As she walked further, her eyes landed on a framed photo of Elias and an unfamiliar woman. She picked it up carefully.

"He looks... happy in this. Way more charming and healthy than he is now," she murmured. *Who is this beside him?*

Gently, she placed the photo back on the table, lost in thoughts.

"Hmm... maybe I can disguise myself and follow him? But that won't be easy. What if he recognizes me? Or senses that someone's tailing him?" Sofia muttered under her breath. *Still, I have to find out who Thomas really is.*

Glancing at Elias, she saw him fast asleep. Fatigue weighed on her as well. With a sigh, she washed the bowl, then lay down on the bed. Sleep didn't come easily—she wasn't used to resting in someone else's home.

The night was quiet, the whole city wrapped in uneasy slumber. It was past 1 AM, and the only sound was the mechanical voice of a patrolling surveillance machine, echoing through the empty streets.

Suddenly, Elias jolted awake. Disoriented, he scanned his surroundings, trying to gauge the time. Squinting at the clock, he saw it was just past 1 AM.

"Ah... why can't I even sleep without these nightmares?" He exhaled sharply, running a hand down his face.

Reaching for his diary, he scribbled down the dream that had wrenched him from sleep:

"Maria came back in the dream. She was knocking on the door. I opened it, and suddenly... I noticed she was holding a knife. She smiled—the eeriest smile I've ever seen—and then... she stabbed me."

Closing the diary, he tucked it into his bag and let out another sigh. His gaze shifted toward Sofia. The dim light softened her features, making her look almost peaceful in her sleep.

"I hope you're sleeping well, Sofia," he whispered, a faint smile touching his lips.

Then his eyes fell on the letter—the one he had written for Maria but never sent. It lay on the table, forgotten yet ever-present.

Every week, he wrote to her. Every week, he slipped the letter into the mailbox, despite never knowing where she was. No address, no certainty it ever reached her. Just a quiet hope that, somehow, it did.

A tear slid down his cheek.

"I don't even feel sleepy... Maybe I should just post the letter," he murmured.

The nearest post box was about 500 meters from his house. With a deep breath, he grabbed the letter and decided to go.

While on his way he was quite lost in thoughts

"Will my plan actually work? My days are numbered. I'm certain things won't go as planned. The confidence with which I told Sofia about my plan... how fearless I pretended to be in the face of death... but in reality, it's the complete opposite."

Elias sighed, tilting his head up to the sky. The stars stretched endlessly above him, more visible than usual in the absence of the moon.

"Life isn't so bad after all... I guess." He kept walking, eyes still on the sky.

Soldiers patrolled the streets, but none stopped him. The local guards within a few kilometers knew who he was. As he passed by a speaking machine, he noticed stacks of newspapers piled up inside, waiting for morning distribution.

Reaching the post box, he hesitated, staring at the letter in his hands. Taking a deep breath, he finally slipped it inside and whispered the same words he always did—*"Maybe someday..."* A tear rolled down his cheek. The memories still felt fresh, yet in reality, they were distant.

Just then, a soldier passed by, humming an old song—a rare sight, as most soldiers preferred the new propaganda tunes. The melody was so soothing that Elias instinctively approached him.

"H-Hey... I liked that song. Do you listen to it often?" Elias asked.

The soldier hesitated before responding. *"E-Elias, right? I've heard about your deeds in the South. It's an honor to meet you. Yeah, I enjoy old songs, but I don't listen to them much. It attracts unnecessary suspicion. But technically, in North Parserland, people are allowed to listen to any kind of music... though, of course, nothing surpasses the songs produced by the Ministry of Songs."*

Elias could sense the soldier's inner rebellion, carefully hidden behind his words. He also noted how the man referenced an old law—one that hadn't been amended yet—which still allowed citizens to listen to any music. But in reality, playing older songs often raised suspicions, especially if one had any prior criminal associations.

Elias smirked slightly. *"Ah, I see."*

The soldier adjusted his rifle. *"I should get going. Have a good night, sir. It's peaceful out here."*

Elias watched him leave. *"Yeah... peaceful,"* he muttered under his breath. *"But who knows what's happening behind our backs?"*

Just after a few steps, Elias heard the clinking noise of steel, as if someone—or several people—were being tied with cuffs, their legs shackled as well.

Hearing the sound, Elias decided to follow it.

It was happening just down the road. Around 10–15 Southern prisoners, barely able to walk, were being forced forward. Soldiers surrounded them, herding them like cattle toward the prison cells.

Elias felt helpless.

All of a sudden, one of the prisoners collapsed, too exhausted to continue. Gasping, he begged for water, saying he couldn't walk any further.

A soldier sneered at him. "You worthless bastard. Weak pig. Insolent scum." Spitting at the man, he kicked him viciously, beating him without restraint.

The other prisoners, watching in silence, didn't dare to ask for anything. They simply dragged their feet forward, knowing stopping meant death.

"Such lazy bastards they are," one soldier laughed

"Indeed, comrade," the one delivering the beating replied.

Elias, watching everything, remained silent. Without drawing attention, he slipped into an abandoned lane. Taking out his camera, he zipped it into his pocket, leaving only the lens exposed to capture the moment

Then, acting as if nothing had happened, he walked past the prisoners, recording everything without raising suspicion.

By the time he reached home, unease crept into his chest. Such acts always made him anxious—what if he got caught? Or worse, what if someone had already noticed?

As he stepped inside ,he took a deep breath, feeling a wave of relief.

Sofia was still asleep. She hadn't woken up or gone looking for him.

Moving as quietly as possible, he shut the door, placed his coat in its usual spot, and took small, steady steps toward the sofa. Lying down, he stared at the ceiling, thinking.

I'll tell Sofia about everything i saw tonight.

XIX

SPEAK SPEAK SPEAK

In the morning, the clock blared again, startling Sofia and scaring her.

"What is this? Why is it speaking?" she exclaimed.

Hearing her, Elias woke up as well.

"Bah, it ain't speaking. It's just an alarm—compulsory in every home in the North," he muttered, forcing himself up from the sofa. He walked towards the clock and turned it off.

"It usually—no, not usually—it always blares the same thing, like a damn parrot. I hate its voice. Can't even break it, you know? Once, a neighbor of mine smashed his out of anger. An alarm went off from inside, and within minutes, soldiers stormed the building. They arrested him for 'disloyalty.'"

Elias sighed. He still felt exhausted, his body aching from wandering all night instead of sleeping.

"You seem tired," Sofia noted. She could see the exhaustion on his face—it had a sickly, yellowish hue.

"Y-yeah, sort of. I went for a, uh... how should I put it? A walk. Yeah, a late-night walk," Elias replied, a bit hesitant. He was unsure whether to tell her about Maria. In the end, he decided not to.

"Oh, I see. But why?" Sofia asked, curious.

"Forget that. Look at this—what I saw last night," Elias said quickly, taking out his camera and connecting it to the screen.

The footage played.

To Elias' surprise, Sofia recognized some of the prisoners.

"They're from the Aviation 5th Battalion. I know them. They were the bravest fighters we had in all of South Parserland..." Her voice trailed off as hopelessness settled deeper within her.

"Ah, so they were from the aviation division," Elias murmured.

"This adds to my evidence, but it won't make much of a difference. Maybe it will, though—seeing how the soldiers spat on that prisoner and kicked him just for asking for water." He paused, knowing that Northerners would likely see such acts as justified against their enemies.

But if he could change even *one* person's mind, it would be a victory.

"I can't believe it... The South is really falling. It's really falling..."

Tears streamed down Sofia's face as the weight of it all crashed over her.

Elias moved quickly to console her, reaching out—

"Don't you dare. Don't you dare come near me," she snapped, reacting from his touch. "Just—just go away. For God's sake... oh wait, I forgot—you have no gods here. So for your leader's sake, please."

Her voice broke, raw with grief.

Elias stood there, helpless. Not a great start to the morning.

He let out a quiet sigh. "Just trust me—only this time."

Without waiting for a response, he picked up a loaf of bread, grabbed his coat, and walked towards the door , however he did not lock it this time.

"Lock it if you want," he said before stepping out.

He had no intention of trapping her, of making her feel like a prisoner in a foreign land. If she wanted to leave, she could without any restrictions.

As he disappeared down the stairs, Sofia wiped her tears, her expression hardening.

"I'll only find peace when I see your downfall, Elias," she muttered under her breath.

And then—suddenly—she remembered. The plan.

Her plan.

To follow Elias.

Her eyes darted to the unlocked door. This was her chance. She could finally slip away and meet Thomas.

Heart pounding, she scanned the house for something to conceal herself. Her gaze landed on Elias' winter scarf. Without hesitation, she wrapped it around her face, leaving only her eyes visible, and quickly tied her hair back.

She moved to the window and peered through the curtains. Elias was still downstairs, speaking to someone.

Good. He hadn't left yet.

She let out a slow breath of relief, then silently stepped outside, closing the door behind her.

Before leaving, she grabbed the lock and secured the door from the outside. Elias wouldn't suspect a thing—he'd assume she stayed inside. And by the time he returned, she'd already be back.

He wouldn't even know she was gone.

Besides, she was certain Elias wouldn't be back anytime soon. The North's strict protocols wouldn't allow him to leave work early, and with the South's aviation forces recently breaching the North's airspace, security had tightened. Work would pile up.

He'd be stuck there for hours and she'd have just enough time to complete her task.

Sofia took small, steady steps downstairs. Midway, it struck her—there was an elevator in the building. Too late now. She sighed.

"How stupidly I think sometimes."

At the exit, she peeked through the door to check if Elias was still occupied. He had finished talking and was now heading toward his office.

"Great." She muttered under her breath.

She followed at a safe distance, keeping her pace natural—far enough not to raise suspicion but close enough to track him. The real risk wasn't Elias noticing her; it was the soldiers. If any of them got suspicious, she'd be done for. But to her surprise, she had already passed a few of them, and not a single one had stopped her or demanded to see her face.

"Perhaps they think I'm sick?"

Elias entered a café to buy a packet of bread—for Jai. The dog was always with him, trailing behind wherever he went. Elias rarely checked on him because Jai had a way of following without being called. A part of him knew he was being negligent, but his mind was too occupied to dwell on it.

Sofia halted, pretending to scan her surroundings, careful not to attract attention.

Then—

A soldier approached her. Young, sharp-featured, with a well-groomed mustache, luxurious blond hair, and piercing blue eyes. His uniform was immaculate, each button perfectly aligned.

"Are you alright, madam? Never seen you around like this," he said, his voice firm but curious.

"A-ah, yes, yes, I've lived here since birth. Just feeling a little sick," she stammered, then quickly steadied herself. "Didn't want others catching it. But I have urgent work at my office, so I have to go."

It sounded natural enough. The soldier didn't seem suspicious.

"Oh. Well, take care." He nodded and walked away.

Sofia let out a slow, relieved breath.

She turned her gaze to the café. Elias was just leaving, tossing pieces of bread in the air to make Jai jump for them. She hadn't lost track of him.

She resumed following, but suddenly—

A group of soldiers marched past her.

Her breath caught in her throat. Their cold, disciplined expressions, the heaviness of their boots against the pavement, the eerie uniformity of their movements—it all sent a jolt of fear through her.

Memories surged.

The civil war.

The Northerners.

The butchering of her parents.

She clenched her fists. No. Not now.

Wiping away a tear before it could betray her, she forced herself to focus. Elias was nearing his office. She had to stay sharp.

From a distance, she watched as he approached the building.

"Hey, Elias."

Thomas stood at the entrance, as usual.

"Ah, Thomas. Well... pretty good so far," Elias replied, keeping his voice calm, measured. No suspicion. No hesitation.

Then, something caught Elias' attention inside the office.

A crowd.

Too many people. Too much noise. Something was wrong.

"What's that?" he asked.

Thomas rolled his eyes. *"Go see for yourself. The mess those bloody Southern bitches created."*

Elias stepped forward.

And then he saw them.

Bodies.

Dozens of them.

People from the office—trampled, crushed in a stampede. Those still alive were mourning the dead, their grief echoing through the space.

Elias' mind reeled.

Misty.

He had left her in that chaos.

A cold wave of guilt flooded over him.

He turned to Thomas, his voice uneasy. *"W-where's Misty?"*

Thomas let out a sigh. *"She's dead too."*

For the first time, Elias saw Thomas look genuinely defeated. His face was tight with suppressed grief, his usual arrogance absent. No wonder—he had always liked Misty. More than his own mistress, even. It was obvious. The way he flirted with her. The way he spoke about her that night.

"She—she died?"

The guilt deepened.

To save one life, he had condemned another.

Misty had done nothing wrong. She wasn't part of this war. She was innocent. And now, she was dead. Because of him.

Hazy memories flashed—

The late-night tea conversations.

The way she teased him.

The way she had clung to his hand in the crowd.

The way she had pleaded. *"Don't leave me."*

And he had.

Elias felt sick. His mind screamed that it wasn't his fault, but his conscience whispered otherwise.

In a surge of emotion, he turned to Thomas. *"I'm sorry, comrade. Maybe... maybe I could've saved her. I was there, in the stampede. I saw her, but the crowd—"* He paused. He couldn't tell the truth. He couldn't mention Sofia. *"I—I could do nothing."*

Why was he saying this?

Why was he explaining himself to Thomas?

Thomas, of all people—his enemy.

Maybe Elias wasn't saying it for Thomas. Maybe he was saying it for himself.

But Thomas' expression darkened.

"Wait... That means you could have saved her?"

His tone sharpened, his hands clenching into fists.

Before Elias could react, Thomas grabbed him by the collar.

"Wish I could give you a tight smack in the face," he muttered through gritted teeth, before releasing him with a frustrated sigh.

Hatred burned in his eyes.

Elias had lost his trust completely.

From a distance, Sofia watched.

She made no move.

But as she saw the stranger gripping Elias by the collar, a thought struck her—

Could that man be Thomas?

She waited until Thomas was alone in that area. It took nearly thirty minutes for the crowd to disperse after the alarm blared, urging workers to return to their duties, also reminding them that mourning would not bring back the dead.

As she took a few steps forward, she noticed Thomas heading back to work—unsurprising, given that he was employed there. Deciding to wait, she crossed the street to the café opposite the office. She was fairly certain that workers would step out during lunch, and if Thomas did not, she could slip inside while the doors remained open. Still, she was unsure if the plan would even work. Yet, turning back to Elias' home empty-handed was not an option. She was determined.

Meanwhile, inside the office, the scene was different. Elias spent his time contemplating how to gather more evidence against the Party. He had no idea what Sofia was up to, nor did he suspect she might be working against him behind his back.

Sofia entered the café only to realize she had no money. A few spare Southern coins clinked in her pocket, but they were of no use here. She wandered around aimlessly, pretending to admire the surroundings while passing the time. The waiters yawned, eyeing her with mild irritation—why was she here if she didn't plan to order? Still, they didn't bother her, too occupied with serving paying customers.

The café owner, a woman—an unusual sight in the North—eventually approached her. "Can I help you with something?"

"N-no, just looking at these paintings. They look great," Sofia replied, trying to avoid suspicion.

"True, they are," the owner said, though her eyes lingered on Sofia's masked face. "Why the mask?" she asked, her tone shifting with suspicion, as though she suspected Sofia of being a thief.

"I'm just sick," Sofia replied curtly, her cold demeanor unsettling the owner.

The woman frowned slightly. "Sorry, but if you're not going to order anything, you'll have to leave," she said with an essence of frustration.

Just then, a speaking machine rolled past the café, blaring an announcement in its usual mechanical voice. The café fell silent as people turned to listen:

"We need you. For your country. For your family. For True Parserland. For one united Parserland. Join the army. The Supreme Leader will be proud of you."

The entire café erupted in perfect unison: "All hail the Supreme Leader!" Not a single voice was out of sync.

Yet Sofia remained silent. Strangely, no one noticed. Her mask concealed her lips, making it impossible to tell whether she had chanted along.

Back at the office, Elias approached the head secretary and inquired whether he had to serve as John's replacement, even for the day. The head informed him of John's detainment—something Elias already knew—but he feigned ignorance. That was the one thing Elias excelled at. He sighed inwardly as the head ordered him to take over

John's duties until a suitable replacement was found.

Elias agreed. The position would allow him to document more people like Mr. Fistros.

Wasting no more time, Elias entered the prison. The stench was still unbearable at first, but he had grown used to it. Pinching his nose briefly, he pressed forward until the smell faded slightly.

The lights flickered overhead. Blood still dripped from the ceiling. In the distance, prisoners' screams echoed through the halls. A lingering mystery gnawed at him—what lay above the Nationalist Department? Why did blood seep through the ceiling? He had never given it much thought before, but now, for the first time, his mind fixated on these questions.

However, he brought all his attention towards the present and started walking further, searching for any other prisoners he could interview. It wouldn't be easy—earlier, Mr. Fistros already knew about Elias, so building trust had been simpler. But now, he had nothing to rely on. Still, he kept moving forward.

He could hear the laughter of soldiers echoing through the halls, a sound that felt almost demonic, as if evils had been sent by their master to haunt this place.

As he walked further, the darkness thickened, forcing him to pull out his small torch. The weak beam cast light in only a small radius, making it difficult to see anything, but it was better than nothing.

Soon, he reached Mr. Fistros' cell, but the darkness was too dense to tell if he was still there. Taking small, steady steps forward, Elias moved closer.

Then, he stepped on something wet.

It felt like water—maybe a leak somewhere. He could hear the faint splash with every step. But just to be sure, he lowered his torch towards the ground.

His breath hitched.

It wasn't water. It was blood. A deep, dark red.

For a moment, panic shot through him. His mind immediately jumped to the worst conclusion—was it Mr. Fistros'? He clenched his fists, forcing himself to stay composed, and stepped forward to see for himself.

What lay before him was unbearable.

Mr. Fistros was dead. His face was nearly severed from the neck, barely hanging on. Blood still poured from his wrists, his arteries cut open just moments ago. His leg—nowhere to be seen.

Elias' stomach twisted. He felt like throwing up, but he swallowed it down. Shaking, he pulled out his recorder, glancing around before hurriedly taking a picture. Then, without wasting a second, he turned and ran.

He didn't dare look back.

Tears streamed down his face.

How could someone do this?

How?

This couldn't be the work of a human. No, it couldn't.

Elias did not run toward the exit but in the opposite direction. Subconsciously, he knew he couldn't leave the cell now—not without raising suspicion. He had just entered. What excuse could he possibly give for leaving so soon?

Eventually, exhaustion caught up with him, and he stopped. He was now deep inside the prison. Out of sheer fatigue, he collapsed onto the floor—only to realize too late that it was drenched in blood.

A river of blood.

He hadn't even noticed that he had been running through it. The splashes had stained his face, seeping into his clothes.

Elias screamed. Loudly.

But no one would hear him. Not here.

The darkness swallowed everything. His torch slipped from his hand, landing in the blood with a faint hiss as it short-circuited.

Panic threatened to consume him. He felt dizzy, his vision blurring. But he forced himself to stand—he had to. If he passed out here, no one would come for him. No one would even know.

Step by step, he moved toward the exit. The air felt suffocating, pressing down on him. His only source of light was gone, and now, he could see nothing.

He cursed himself for being careless with the torch.

Now, there was only darkness.

He kept walking in the opposite direction from where he had come.

At this point, he felt as though he had already died. Or if he wasn't dead, he might as well pay someone to kill him and end it all.

He shut his eyes, unable to bear the horrific sights around him, and continued walking forward, straight ahead.

Then, a faint memory surfaced.

The same memory from when he had been unconscious in the truck, coming back *to the North from the South.*

The snow. The graves of his friends lined up in a row.
The stormy winds.
The undead memories of the civil war, now permanently etched into his mind.

But this time, it was different. The door he saw now was more defined—more like an actual door—casting a faint white glow around it. It stood just behind the graves, an eerie presence in the desolate scene.

Subconsciously, he moved toward it. And then—he opened his eyes.

The vision dissolved, replaced by reality. He was at the exit of the prison cell. A deep breath escaped him as he took in his surroundings.

The soldiers stationed at the exit turned toward him. Elias stood before them, drenched in blood—his face, his clothes, everything soaked in crimson. For a moment, they didn't recognize him.

"Who are you?" one of them asked.

Elias scoffed. "Elias. Or who else could I be?" His voice carried frustration, exhaustion.

The soldier exhaled, shaking his head. "What a mess inside."

"Well, you can't go out looking like that." Another soldier gestured to the left. "Not the first time an employee's walked out of there like this. There's a changing room—spare clothes. Use them."

They rolled their eyes as Elias walked off, muttering under their breaths. Another one.

The blood had dried, making his clothes cling to his skin like a second layer of flesh. Peeling them off was painful. He stank—like a rotting corpse, if he had to describe it.

When he stepped out of the dressing room, only his clothes had changed. He'd washed his face, but the stench of blood still clung to him. Yet, the fresh clothes made him feel marginally better—less like a walking carcass.

"See? Good as new," a soldier remarked.

Elias sighed, contemplating whether to go back inside the cell or not. Before he could decide, the lunch bell blared across the facility. A welcome distraction.

Without a second thought, he turned on his heels and headed straight for the canteen, ignoring everything and everyone around him. He didn't look for colleagues, didn't seek conversation—he just wanted to get away from that place, even if only for a while.

Sofia heard the lunch bell too. She was still lingering outside the café, where the owner had rudely dismissed her.

Excitement flickered inside her. It was almost time to see Thomas.

She scanned the crowd leaving the office building, searching for him. But a new problem dawned on her—what if he was eating in the canteen? She had no ID. No way to get in. Her plan was falling apart before it had even begun.

But fate had its own design.

Grieving Misty's death, Thomas chose to step outside for lunch, needing fresh air.

And then—Sofia spotted him. Or at least, she thought it was him. Without hesitation, she rushed toward him, gripping her scarf to keep it from blowing off and revealing her face.

Thomas saw the figure darting toward him, covered in a scarf, and his body tensed.

An assassin? he thought. *No, those don't exist anymore... do they?*

Sofia stopped near him, breathless.

"Who are you, comrade?" Thomas asked with a smirk, eyes narrowing. He could tell—just by the way she carried herself—she was a woman. And that only made him more curious.

"That's a matter for later," Sofia said between breaths. "I have vital information about Elias."Thomas blinked. "Elias?" His gaze flickered around, checking if Elias—or anyone else—was nearby.

"Come to my cabin," he said in a low voice. "Talk there, or someone will hear."

Sofia hesitated but finally nodded. "Y-yes."

"Follow me."

She trailed behind him into the office. The moment she stepped inside, she froze.

Propaganda posters loomed over the walls. Red flags draped across the space. The air was thick with the suffocating presence of the Party.

Sofia swallowed hard.

She had spent her life fighting against this regime. And now, she was inside its heart.

People looked at her—confused, curious—wondering about the scarf wrapped tightly around her face. Sofia avoided their eyes, silently praying she wouldn't bump into Elias. There was still a chance he might recognise her.

"Here's my cabin," Thomas said, stepping aside.

Sofia quickly slipped inside, her pace startling him for a moment. But he didn't say anything. He shut the door behind them.

She let out a deep breath, feeling a strange sense of safety now that only Thomas could hear her.

"You can take off your mask if you want," Thomas said, half-questioning.

"N-no," she fumbled. Her thoughts tangled. Should she show her face? What if he recognised her as the prisoner from the South—the one who'd escaped? If he worked for the Party, then surely he knew someone had survived the stampede.

Thomas rolled his eyes. "Well? Speak, then. I'm literally giving you my lunch break here—and I'm starving like a bear," he sighed.

"Yes," she began, trying to gather confidence, "I heard you have a personal grievance against Elias. So do I. We both have a common enemy. If we work together, Elias's downfall is inevitable—I can assure you that."

Thomas raised an eyebrow. "Fair enough. But what is it that you know? What do you have against Elias?"

Sofia leaned forward, her voice low. "He's conspiring something big against the Party. He's gathering evi—"

Her words were cut off by a sharp knock on the door. Both she and Thomas froze.

"Comrade? I brought you tea. Still working? Didn't you hear it's lunchtime?"

It was Josh—Thomas's friend—knocking cheerfully on the door, expecting it to open.

"I—I ought to hide," Sofia whispered, panic rising. The voice from outside had, for a moment, sounded like Elias's.

Without waiting for Thomas, she crawled beneath the table.

"Why are you hiding now?" Thomas groaned under his breath. Her paranoia was starting to wear on him.

"Yes, comrade—opening," Thomas called out, trying to sound casual. He opened the door and let Josh in.

"Comrade, here's the tea. All hail the Supreme Leader! Did you hear? Tea prices are dropping by 10%," Josh said, grinning.

"True. Can't thank the Supreme Leader enough," Thomas replied with a hearty laugh. "Now we can have tea peacefully, even at midnight."

But inwardly, he wished Josh would leave already.

"Lunch? Won't you eat? Come, let's go to the canteen," Josh offered.

"Not today, comrade. Too much work piled up. I'd rather finish it now," Thomas said quickly.

"I'll join you this evening—with some booze or beer, eh?" Thomas added with a smile.

"Sounds great, eh?" Josh said, walking out of the cabin.

The moment he left, Thomas rushed to shut the door.

Sofia peeked out from under the table, then stood up. "I thought it was Elias... that's why I hid," she said, brushing herself off.

"Nah, it was just my comrade Josh," Thomas replied, shaking his head.

"Can you *please* be quick now?" he added, impatience written all over his face.

Sofia nodded. "Elias is conspiring against the Party. Something big. But I'll only tell you everything if you promise me a position in the Party."

Thomas gave a short laugh. "Aha! People who expose traitors within the Party are often rewarded. The Secretary himself might give you something."

He leaned in slightly, lowering his tone. "But it *has* to be true. If you lie or exaggerate—even a little—they'll lock you back in the cell. No second chances."

Sofia hesitated. The word 'cell' struck her like a jolt. Her mind flashed back to the clip Elias had shown her that morning.

"What happened? Speak," Thomas asked, his voice low but firm.

"Y-yes," Sofia replied, still fumbling for words.

"He's gathering evidence against the Party... and he plans to present it during the ceremony—when his so-called 'deeds' are being celebrated in front of the citizens," she said, her voice now steady. Deep down, she felt she was avenging the South... the death of their leaders, their voices silenced.

Thomas's eyes widened. "Oh my—he is? *Really?* This would destroy his entire career, if what you say is true. How's that even possible? I didn't get a single hint of what he was doing... sure, he'd rant sometimes when he was drunk, say a few bitter things when he was angry—but *this*? To go this far?"

He paused, processing it.

"If this is true... I assure you, you'll be rewarded. A great place in the Party awaits you. The Supreme Leader himself will be proud of you," he added, eyes gleaming with excitement.

"Wait... what's your name again?" Thomas asked, suddenly curious.

"Sofia," she answered plainly.

"Hm. Sofia... that sounds familiar. Have I heard it recently?" he muttered, half to himself. "Never mind."

He smiled, nodding with approval. "Thank you, Sofia. You're doing a great service—as a true northern citizen should. *This* is loyalty. This is what we need for our Supreme Leader. Not like those filthy Southerns," he sneered.

Sofia clenched her fists. Her nails dug into her palms—but she controlled herself.

"I–I'll be going now," said Sofia and walked off the room.

Her mind was muddled. Had she done the right thing—or stepped into the wrong? She couldn't tell. But somewhere within, a burden felt lifted. The party was behind her now—something Elias didn't have anymore.

Inside the room, Thomas was burning with rage. Not at Sofia, but at himself—for being blind to everything happening behind the party's back. And yet, he couldn't confront Elias outright. Elias worked in the nationalist department—one couldn't simply throw accusations there. He needed proof. He had to catch him red-handed.

Still, Thomas couldn't hide the grin spreading across his face. His mind was already racing towards the secretary's office. His promotion seemed like a done deal.

"Ah... what to do with Sofia then?" he muttered, shrugging.

"Give her a small position. Maybe paperwork. Something trivial." He chuckled to himself.
"I'll take all the credit anyway. Just tell them she helped a bit, so she doesn't make a scene in front of the secretary."

Meanwhile, Sofia had already made up her mind. She would go straight to Elias' home—to keep her cover intact, to avoid any flicker of suspicion.

She even spotted Elias at the gate while leaving. But he didn't notice her—his ears were glued to the radio near the entrance, which was blaring the latest war updates. He looked preoccupied, almost dazed.

Sofia quickened her pace and let out a sigh of relief as she stepped out of the building, walking toward the direction from where she had come.

Inside the canteen, Elias sat alone—still faintly stinking, his clothes slightly off despite the change. Confidence didn't accompany him today. Misty's death, the cell experience, the smell of blood—it all weighed on him. Yet the memory of Misty had already begun to fade, buried under the weight of everything else.

With no friend to speak to, Elias chewed in silence. The food was bland, as always—smelled faintly of petrol. But he no longer reacted. He was getting used to it.

Then came the shrill bell and an announcement:
"Lunch break has ended. All comrades are requested to

return to their work within ten minutes. And don't forget to thank the Supreme Leader for the delicious canteen lunch."

Elias sighed, got up, placed his empty utensil in the basin, and washed his hands. People around him gave odd glances, wrinkling their noses at the smell still lingering around him. It made him feel small for a moment, a bit insecure.

But he didn't care. Not today.

He quietly walked back to his work area, gathering whatever scraps of courage still remained inside him.

If readers are wondering where Jai was all this time—Elias had been asked to keep him in a separate room before entering the cell, due to security regulations. He would only be allowed to take him back once he was ready to leave the office—perhaps in the evening.

Elias finally reached the nationalist department again. His eyes lingered on the rusted cell entry door. He stood there for a moment, hesitant... but determined. He had to find more evidence.

He stepped inside, the stench hitting him again, yet his focus remained on one thing—proof. If only he had access to the floor upstairs, he often thought, he might uncover more. Something always bothered him—those blood drops that dripped from the ceiling... where did they come from?

"Welcome back, Elias," the soldiers greeted.

He nodded and waved in return, walking deeper inside.

Meanwhile, Sofia reached Elias' home without drawing much attention—or at least, that's what she believed. One or two soldiers who had seen her heading in that direction earlier might have wondered about her identity, but seeing her come and go from the same path made them dismiss any suspicion. She didn't seem hostile enough.

Inside, she was still conflicted. She kept telling herself she did it for the South—for revenge—for their fallen leaders. But inside... guilt pricked her. Elias had helped her. He had saved her life. And this was how she repaid him?

No. She shook her head, brushing the thought away.

Unwrapping the scarf from her head, Sofia wandered into the kitchen area, checking the fridge. It barely had anything—just some old bread and a few vegetables. She decided to make a sandwich. She had no money to go downstairs and eat anyway.

Back in the cell, Elias trying not to get lost this time.

He met another prisoner. A southerner. Captured during the recent battle.

The man's condition was no different from Fistros—skin peeled, bloodied, broken. Yet somehow... still alive. Still breathing. Still waiting for death.

He couldn't speak. So Elias simply took a photo. One more proof.

His plan was unfolding better than he expected.

He met more prisoners. Some could speak. Some couldn't. He documented whatever he could—capturing images, recording quiet testimonies. Hours passed. The stench clung to his skin. His body began to fail him. He was close to fainting.

And then the final bell rang—the end of the workday.

Without wasting a second, Elias rushed out of the cell, the stale air clinging to his clothes. The first thing he did—was go free Jai.

"Good boy," Elias smiled weakly. "Hope you didn't do any mischief in there?"

Jai sniffed the strange, awful smell coming from him but wagged his tail nonetheless.

A soldier reminded Elias to return the uniform he wore after washing and leave it in the changing room.

"Got it," Elias nodded, then made his way downstairs—ready to leave the building.

But fate wasn't done testing him yet.

Thomas stood near the stairs—and gave him a strange look.

Elias saw it—but kept walking.

"What's in your bag?" Thomas called out, stopping him.

Elias froze.

Why the bag?

Did he know something? Was this it? Was his plan exposed?

"It's... nothing," Elias said, trying to keep his voice steady. "Just office files. What else could be in here?"

He walked past, trying to act normal.

"Will see about that," Thomas muttered, brushing past him with narrowed eyes.

That single sentence echoed in Elias' head like a warning bell.

Am I exposed?

And just then—another voice stopped him.

It was the Secretary Head.

Elias froze again.

Did *he* know too? Was the entire office aware? Were they only pretending?

The Secretary gave him a wide smile. "Your ceremony is scheduled for the day after tomorrow. Be ready with your speech. We're very proud of what you did in the South," he laughed heartily, his stomach jiggling as he laughed.

Elias let out a deep sigh of relief.

He didn't know.

No one did.

"Consider it done, comrade," Elias replied, his voice calm—but his heart racing.

XX

Blindfold

Elias' heart was thumping—his days in this world were now countable. He knew once he showed those clips, he would be shot then and there. The question kept haunting him: was the sacrifice worth it? He was living a decent life just by affirming whatever the Party said. But even that life felt like a prison—no freedom at all.

Maybe... if his sacrifice sparked a civil war in the North, or at least made the people aware of the regime's true face, then perhaps—just perhaps—he'd pat himself from heaven.

He began to whistle an old song. The same one he used to sing with Maria, back when they were newly wed, walking down the streets hand in hand. His eyes filled up with tears.

"Wish you were here..." he whispered.

Just then, a speaking machine blared past him:

"Abandon the old, embrace the new! Listen to the all-new Supreme Leader Song Series 101. Switch your radio to 68.9 Hz and hear the best music! All hail the Supreme Leader!"

"Now what? The next thing they'll announce is that old songs are banned," Elias gritted his teeth, clenching his fists.

Brushing off the frustration, he headed home. He wasn't sure whether Sofia had already left or not. He clearly remembered how he left the door unlocked, and in anger, had said a thing or two he now regretted. He didn't wanted to make her feel uncomfortable. A sigh escaped his lips as he fed Jai the food he'd bought earlier.

The setting sun cast a beautiful glow across the city. Even the building rubbles looked better beneath the orange hues. Birds filled the sky with their chirruping, and the smell of freshly cooked food from a nearby restaurant drifted into the streets.

Perhaps the world starts looking prettier when death feels near, Elias thought. He stopped by a convenience store and bought a cigarette. He barely smoked, but today had been unbearable. His head ached from everything that had happened.

He looked down at Jai and smiled faintly.

"Perhaps you'll have to find a new master soon enough."

A tear dropped from his eye. He had already accepted his death. And why shouldn't he? The ceremony would be packed with soldiers. He would be executed the moment those clips played.

As he approached his apartment, he stood there for a few minutes, just staring at it in silence. He didn't think much—he just looked. Then, instead of taking the lift, he climbed the stairs slowly, wanting to spend a little more time in the building he had called home.

Seeing the door locked from inside gave him a small sense of happiness—Sofia was still there. At least he wouldn't have to face these last days completely alone.

He knocked on the door.

Sofia, who had fallen asleep hungry, jolted awake. There was barely anything in the fridge that suited her—she was a bit of a picky eater, after all.

Startled by the knock, she rubbed her eyes and walked toward the door.

"So you didn't leave, after all," Elias smirked, trying to mask his emotions behind the same brave front he had shown that morning.

"How come he's so calm? Didn't Thomas do anything about him after what I told him? Or... maybe he's still gathering more evidence?" she wondered, confused by Elias' expression.

"Did you eat anything?" Elias asked.

"N-No, not for dinner. But I did have some lunch," Sofia replied.

"Ah, I see. Well, I'm not really in the mood to cook right now—too tired, perhaps," Elias said with disappointment written all over his face.

"Well, you stink today too. Maybe consider taking a shower, rolling her eyes.

"Ah, yeah, yeah..." Elias replied with a sigh.

"Though I do have a few sweet breads in my bag—here," he added, tossing them to her.

"You're not eating anything?" she asked.

"Not hungry," Elias replied with his usual dull tone. He looked thinner than he did back when he first arrived in the South.

He headed to the washroom to take a shower before bed.

Sofia quickly ate the bread—she was hungrier than she let on. She didn't express it, but the way she devoured the food showed it clearly.

Elias came out wearing a towel. The shower had only lasted a few minutes—he wasn't in the mood but had forced himself anyway. Seeing Sofia asleep already, he was surprised. She had eaten and dozed off so fast. A faint smile curled on his lips—her small habits sometimes reminded him of Maria.

He changed into something more comfortable, ready to sleep, but sleep didn't come. His mind was restless—thoughts swirling in chaos, his head pounding from everything he had gone through.

He sat at his desk, where a small window opened to the outside world. The moonlight spilled in gently, offering a strange comfort. He reached for a blank sheet of paper and began writing another letter to Maria—perhaps his last. Who knew what would happen tomorrow?

His hands trembled, but he still tried to write something. He couldn't.

Instead, tears welled up and spilled onto the page.

"Why am I like this? Why is my life like this?" he whispered to himself.

Suddenly, the window turned completely white. He couldn't see anything outside. A figure slowly emerged from the brightness, walking towards him. She was dressed in white, one hand stretched forward as if asking him to come with her, the other resting behind her.

As the figure came closer, Elias's eyes widened.

It was Maria.

He gasped. "Maria... Maria—it's you! It's really you! I finally found you!"

Maria had a gentle smile on her face, one that immediately calmed him from within. The headache that had been tormenting him vanished the moment he saw her.

"You've seen enough, Elias. I can't see you like this anymore. I love you," she said softly.

"You... you love me?" Elias repeated, barely believing his ears. He hadn't heard those words since the day he lost her in the civil war. His eyes brimmed with tears again, overflowing onto the letter he never got to write. It was as if someone had poured an entire river over that piece of paper.

But before he could say more, the figure began to fade.

"No, no! Don't leave me—not yet! Please! Please don't!" he begged, sobbing as he tried to reach out, fumbling.

But the figure disappeared completely, right in front of his eyes.

He suddenly jolted awake.

It had been a hallucination.

Or maybe a dream.

The paper still lay in front of him. The window was just a window again. Outside, it was quiet. No figure, no light.

He turned to see Sofia—still sleeping peacefully.

And once again... he was alone.

He just stared at the sky for almost an hour. It was calming—the stars, the moon straight from the window—it all looked unreal. The small yet gentle clouds... the distant hum of speaking machines roaming through the city. It didn't sound harsh today. In fact, for Elias, it added a strange touch of comfort, a reminder that he wasn't alone.

"What next?" he muttered.

He sighed, got up from the chair, and lay down on the bed, closing his eyes and trying to sleep.

And in no time... it was morning.

The clock blared loudly. He had barely slept a few hours.

Tired, Elias got up to stop the clock. Even Sofia jolted awake from the sudden noise.

"You can sleep," Elias said while getting ready for the office.

"No, I don't feel sleepy," she replied.

"What's your plan today?" asked Sofia.

Elias hesitated a bit, unsure whether he should tell her or not—but finally decided to. He had no idea what she had been doing behind his back, and maybe, just maybe, a bit of trust could grow between them if he shared the truth.

"Well, I recorded quite a good number of interviews and pictures yesterday... so today I'll be transferring them into tape recorders," Elias said, trying to sound confident in front of her.

"Oh, I see. And when's the ceremony?" Sofia asked.

"Tomorrow," he sighed.

Wait... isn't it August?

It should've started snowing by now.

(Weather conditions in Parserland were far different than the real world.)

Elias rushed to the window. Maybe it had snowed while he was sleeping?

He opened the window—and yes. A thin blanket of snow covered the city. Not too much, but enough to cover the streets and roofs. A light snowfall, quiet and soft.

"Woah—see this," Elias called out. For once, his voice had a hint of excitement. Maybe it was his inner child peeking through after so long.

Sofia rubbed her eyes and walked over, still half-asleep.

"Oh yeah... snow. In the South, it snows a month later," she replied lazily.

"Is it so?" Elias wondered.

"Well, I'm getting late for office. Goodbye," he said, grabbing his coat and signaling Jai to follow.

And with that, he rushed out.

He left the door open again. He didn't even bother to check it. His mind was somewhere else now.

Sofia smirked.

Elias Vyane... sadly, you won't even be remembered.

A creepy smile formed on her face—anyone who saw her like that in that moment would've been scared. The way she widened her face while grinning... something about it felt off.

Elias reached the ground floor. He looked at Jai.

"Let's race," he said.

And just like that, he was doing things he used to love as a child.

The city was quiet. Only the usual office workers heading to their departments, and shopkeepers opening their shutters. Speaking machines blaring propaganda, as always.

Still, somehow... it felt quieter and prettier than before.

Elias was constantly trying to distract his mind, but questions kept pouring in.

How will I convert those recordings into tape? What if they send me into the cell again?

The normal office section had those machines, yes—but the cells didn't.

He felt a wave of anxiety creep over him. His head was full of doubts, of calculations, of worry. The plan was shaping itself in his head, but the uncertainty of how he'd execute it was eating away at him.

In no time, he reached the bakery—his usual stop to buy food for Jai.

He would've passed by it entirely had Jai not barked and tugged at his leg. Elias snapped out of his thoughts.

"Ah... right," he whispered.

He looked down at Jai, guilt silently rising inside him.

Jai was innocent—just a good soul. No secrets. No betrayals. He didn't deserve to lose another master.

Elias knelt down beside him, patting his head with a faint, broken smile.

He bought him the best food available—the most expensive one. Perhaps this would be his last time feeding Jai. That thought alone stung him more than anything else.

After a short walk, Elias finally reached the office.

He stopped. Stared at the building for a minute.

Then entered.

As always, Thomas was standing at the door.

"Elias!" Thomas called out sharply.

But this time, Elias didn't stop. He didn't even look up. He just lowered his head and walked past him silently.

The Secretary Head happened to be entering the building right beside him. He noticed Elias and said in a very firm tone, "Wait right there."

Elias paused, startled for a second.

"We've found an alternative to John," the Secretary said. "So just go back to your regular post."

Elias blinked.

Maybe—just maybe—the universe *wanted* him to carry out this plan. Just minutes ago, he was wondering how he'd execute it if stuck inside the cells again. And now, here it was—an open door.

With John's replacement found, Elias could now access the machines again.

He could continue—pretending it was just... office work.

XXI

SMILE

(This is the last chapter of Blind Patriot. I, the author, would like to thank you from the bottom of my heart for taking your precious time to read this book till here. Cheers—and keep reading!)

Elias rushed to the second floor, repeatedly pressing the elevator button, more frantic than ever before. He was in a hurry like never before. It would be easier to convert those files now—before the office got crowded. People were still arriving, so he wouldn't draw much attention.

From a distance, Thomas noticed his behavior.
"What a lunatic," he chuckled, shaking his head.

The elevator finally arrived. Elias stepped in quickly and shut the door before anyone else could enter.

My plan is working... the universe is with me... the— he paused mid-thought, searching for the right words.
The South is with me... he whispered under his breath as the elevator climbed to the second floor.

When the door opened, Elias immediately spotted a few employees already around, more than he had expected. Still, to avoid suspicion, he composed himself and walked calmly towards the machine, acting like it was just another day.

And slowly, carefully... he made his way toward it.

He inserted the memory card from his camera. The machine came to life, humming and creaking with the sound of its old engine. It hadn't been used in a while, so its noise attracted attention. Some workers nearby turned, curious—why was Elias using that?

The screen displayed: **"Please wait 15 minutes. Video tapes will be ejected shortly."**

One of Elias' colleagues approached, curiosity written all over his face.

"What are you working on? It's unusual to see anyone using this thing these days."

Elias wasn't expecting the interruption and fumbled a bit. But he quickly pulled himself together.

"A-ah... well," he shrugged, "I don't know myself. Got orders to convert a few clips into tapes and submit them." He tried to sound casual.

"Ah, I see. Well... nice to see this old thing still working like a charm," the colleague said.

"True indeed," Elias replied, forcing a smile.

Just then, the office bell rang. Everyone scurried to their seats. Elias stayed back, standing nervously by the machine. A small tremor passed through him. *What if the Secretary Head walks in? He never ordered this task...*

The machine suddenly stopped.

Panic surged inside Elias.

Why? What happened? Is it broken?

Then—*clack!*

The output compartment ejected the video tapes with a mechanical snap.

Elias let out a deep breath of relief. The clips were there—real, tangible, in his hands. He could already imagine the rebellion they would trigger, the storm they'd unleash. His only wish now... that they would work just as planned tomorrow during the ceremony.

He clutched the tapes and quickly returned to his desk before anyone else came snooping. Jai was beside him—loyal as ever. He was only barred from the prison cell, not the rest of the office, so he quietly sat with Elias as usual.

Elias resumed his regular work. His hands moved, but his mind wasn't present. Inside him danced a mix of excitement and fear—the fear of death that awaited him tomorrow, and the excitement of a rebellion he would never live to see. He was sure of it—he'd be shot the moment the tape began to play. But it wouldn't stop right away. The screen would continue flashing the truth for everyone to see... and maybe, just maybe, the people would finally understand what Parserland had become.

Evening came quickly.

Just as Elias began packing his things, ready to head home and finally rest—

The radio crackled to life with an announcement.

"All citizens are to work overtime today. New mandate from the Central Committee. Dismissal only after 11 PM."

Elias dropped his shoulders in exhaustion.

He was disappointed. He had wanted to share everything with Sofia that night—how his plan was working, how close they were to the spark of something big.

Still, he worked. So did everyone else. The entire office looked worn out, their faces tired and blank. But Elias... he was different. He was tired, yes—but something still kept him going.

His eyes kept drifting between his desk and the clock. Every minute dragged like an hour. His fingers were barely able to type. At one point, he was so slow that one of his colleagues snapped at him for not doing his job properly. But how could he explain that he hadn't slept last night? That his mind was already in a battlefield?

The last thirty minutes felt like thirty hours.

Finally—*ding*—it was 11 PM.

Jai had fallen asleep beneath the desk. At Elias' soft whistle, the dog immediately stood up, wagging his tail, alert and loyal.

Elias packed his bag, slipped the tapes inside, and began walking toward the exit.

I wonder what Sofia's doing now... Probably asleep, he thought.

As soon as he stepped outside the building, a harsh gust of wind slammed into him. Snow was everywhere—thick and heavy. Buildings weren't even fully visible anymore. The storm was strong tonight.

He reached for his torch... and then remembered—it had short-circuited back in the cell. He never replaced it.

Frustrated, Elias kicked the wall beside him in anger—only to wince in pain.

"Why always me?!" he muttered bitterly.

Then, to his relief, he saw a group near the entrance distributing oil lamps to employees heading home. Elias rushed to grab one.

"Hey, comrade—return that tomorrow, alright?" said the man handing them out.

Elias tipped his hat as a sign of respect. "Yes, I will. Don't worry."

The man smiled at his gesture, and Elias began his long, cold walk home.

The wind was picking up again, so he picked up his pace. Streetlamps flickered through the snowy fog, casting strange, dreamy shadows. The wind whispered past the buildings, swirling around Elias like ghosts of the past.

He held the lamp in front of him, its glow faint but enough to guide him. He walked alone, speaking to the wind as if it were a friend walking beside him.

His mind replayed thoughts of the upcoming civil war, the consequences of that clip—the one he had just spent days creating. The clip that would cost him everything. His life. His future.

He pulled the file from his bag and looked at it under the lamp's light, his eyes shining with excitement—and tears.

"This... this will ignite the revolution. The revolution I always waited for. We waited for," he whispered to himself.

Then—

"Elias Vyane."

A sharp voice called from behind.

Elias startled. He almost dropped the file.

It was too dark—the lamp couldn't cast far enough. All he saw was a vague silhouette. The figure stepped closer.

"Elias Vyane!" the voice repeated, louder now.

Elias' spine stiffened. The voice sent chills through him. "Wh-who is it?" he asked, fumbling. Seeing this , Jai started to bark loudly.

"It's me, comrade... me," the figure replied, laughing darkly.

As the figure stepped into the glow of the lamp, Elias' heart dropped.

"Thomas," he said, forcing a laugh—pretending to be calm.

"I know what you're holding," Thomas smirked. "I know everything."

Elias' eyes widened. His body froze. He couldn't speak, but his pale face said it all.

Thomas pulled out a pistol and pointed it at him.

"Give it to me. Now. Or I swear I'll shoot—and your so-called revolution will die, just like the rest of those filthy Southerners," he said coldly.

Seeing this, Jai attacked Thomas, but Thomas swiftly freed himself because Jai was not a particularly big or ferocious dog, and flung him to the left, injuring Jai and knocking him unconscious.

Elias knew it was over. If he handed it over, he'd still be reported. There was no escape. Death stood in front of him now—whether by bullet, or in the same prison cell where Fistros was butchered.

"Just shoot me, you coward bitch!" Elias screamed, spitting on the ground.

"Not so easily, comrade. Not so easily," Thomas chuckled, dark and evil.

"The soldiers are already on their way. You know how it is. The Supreme Leader always knows who is where, and where is who. For me, the Party comes first—above everything. I will peel the skin off every traitor of this nation. You included."

Elias dropped the file on the snow-covered road. The wind grew stronger. A few flakes landed on the tapes.

"Put the lamp down—and your hands up!" Thomas barked.

Elias obeyed.

"But how did you know?" Elias asked, his voice shaking. "You knew all along? Then why didn't you catch me back in the cell?"

Thomas chuckled. "Elias Vyane. You think I'm stupid? Sure, I could've caught you back then. But I knew you'd record even more people. Now I've got more proof—enough to bury you forever. You've got no escape."

"And how? You don't even work in the Nationalist Department," Elias whispered.

"Aha... meet my new friend. Or should I say—your old one."

Footsteps echoed from behind.

Elias turned.

Sofia.

"You! Why?" he broke into tears. "I did this for you... for your South. I wanted your people to win. Why would you do this?"

He fell to his knees. The pain in his chest too sharp to stand. His words echoed in the silent night.

"Why...?"

Sofia stepped closer. Her voice was cold, almost unrecognizable now.

"You were too foolish, Elias," she said. "All I ever wanted from the start was power. It's all a game of power. Who doesn't want power? The citizens... they're nothing more than pawns in this game."

Elias looked up at her, broken. The wind howled around them, but her words cut deeper than any storm ever could.

From a distance, the sound of marching soldiers began to grow louder.

Thomas and Sofia stood there—laughing.

Their laughter echoed across the snowy street, louder and louder.

And in that laugh—

No one could tell...

Who was from the North,

And who from the South.

THE END